The Unquiet Past

KELLEY ARMSTRONG

ORCA BOOK PUBLISHERS

Library and Archives Canada Cataloguing in Publication

Armstrong, Kelley, author
The unquiet past / Kelley Armstrong.
(Secrets)

Issued in print, electronic and audio disc formats.
ISBN 978-1-4598-0654-2 (pbk.).—ISBN 978-1-4598-0657-3 (pdf).—
ISBN 978-1-4598-0658-0 (epub).—ISBN 978-1-4598-1088-4 (audio disc)

I. Title. II. Series: Secrets (Victoria, B.C.)
PS8551.R7637U57 2015   jc813'.6   C2015-901750-5
C2015-901751-3
C2015-901752-1

First published in the United States, 2015
Library of Congress Control Number: 2015935515

Summary: In this paranormal YA thriller, Tess embarks on a quest to find out the truth about her parents and realizes that she possesses unusual powers that link her to the past.

Orca Book Publishers is dedicated to preserving the environment and has printed this book on Forest Stewardship Council® certified paper.

Orca Book Publishers gratefully acknowledges the support for its publishing programs provided by the following agencies: the Government of Canada through the Canada Book Fund and the Canada Council for the Arts, and the Province of British Columbia through the BC Arts Council and the Book Publishing Tax Credit.

Cover design by Teresa Bubela
Front cover image by iStockphoto.com; back cover images by Shutterstock.com
Author photo by Kathryn Hollinrake

ORCA BOOK PUBLISHERS
www.orcabook.com

Printed and bound in Canada.

18   17   16   15   •   5   4   3   2

For Julia

The distinction between past, present and future is only a stubbornly persistent illusion.
—Albert Einstein

One

TESS SNEAKED OUT of the orphanage a couple of hours before dawn. That was the best time to meet Billy—even on a Sunday he needed to deliver the bread before six. As Tess's dreams got worse, she found herself getting up earlier and earlier anyway, so she was happy for the excuse to avoid sleep.

The smell of freshly baked bread led her across the town park. As she drew near, Billy held out a hunk of it, letting wisps of cinnamon and yeast waft her way.

"Works better than a trail of bread crumbs," he said.

"Tastes better too," she said as she took a bite.

The orphanage never got the cinnamon-raisin loaves. Mrs. Hazelton—the matron—said it wasn't healthy. It tasted healthy enough to Tess.

"Mom mixed in extra cinnamon for you," Billy said.

Tess mumbled her thanks through a mouthful of bread. His mom wouldn't have said outright that she'd done that for Tess. No one was supposed to know they were meeting in the middle of the night. Everyone did anyway. It was the worst-kept secret in Hope, and for good reason.

Tess had first seen Billy in town over a decade ago, but she'd only really met him five years later, when she'd been put in charge of bakery runs. Actually, that had been another girl's job, but Tess had bribed her into switching. Her scheme had worked for two years, until the matron realized Tess had almost every job that involved going to town. It wasn't that there was much to see in Hope—it was just a change of scenery, and Tess's soul ached for change of any sort.

Tess and Billy had become friends. There'd been hints that he wanted to be more until last summer, when he met a boy at camp and figured out why he'd never actually tried to kiss Tess. She'd been relieved. She didn't think of him "that way" and had been dreading his overture. Now, to keep his secret, they met a couple of nights a week, and everyone in town assumed they were dating.

That suited Tess just fine. Whenever she started thinking one of the local boys was growing up awfully cute, she reminded herself of Cricket, an older girl at the Home. Cricket used to keep scrapbooks of all the places she wanted to see once she turned eighteen and left the orphanage. Then she met a boy who wanted to stay in Hope, and now Tess would see her out walking their baby and watching the train bound for Toronto. In just over a year, Tess would turn eighteen, and she'd be on that train. She wasn't letting anything—even cute boys—stop her.

"Mom told me to give these to you," Billy said as they settled onto the dew-damp grass. He passed her a paper bag. "Suze left them behind when she went to college."

Tess opened the bag and gasped. She reverently pulled out a glossy copy of *Vogue*. Last summer, Tess had "accidentally" ripped one of her skirts and altered it into a mini. Just being frugal. Mrs. Hazelton hadn't been fooled; she'd bought her a new long skirt and left Tess to dream of minis and knee-high boots.

"They're a little old," Billy said. The magazines were dated 1963—last year.

"They're newer than anything I have. Thank you. Tell Suze I'll sew her a—" Tess caught a whiff of something on the breeze. "Do you smell that?"

"Might be sourdough rye. Mom was going to try a new recipe."

"No, it smells like…"

Tess scrambled to her feet. Smoke. She smelled smoke. Beside her, Billy rose, saying, "Something's on fire."

He wheeled toward the town. She looked toward the imposing manor that had been her home for as long as she could remember. The Benevolent Home for Necessitous Girls. Smoke curled from two second-story windows.

Tess dropped the bread and ran.

Fire. The house was on fire. As Tess raced back to it, that's all she could think.

My home is on fire.

There were no flames yet. But that smoke meant flames were coming, and she had to get up there, wake the others, make sure everyone got out.

As soon as she neared the house, she realized no one needed her to raise the alarm. The procedure for a fire had been drilled into all of them, and the older girls were getting the younger ones onto the main level and checking to be sure everyone was there. When they discovered Tess was missing, one of the girls might go back upstairs and try to find her. A friend risking her life for Tess, because she wasn't where she was supposed to be. Because she'd snuck out. Again.

Tess yanked open the side door without even checking to see if the handle was hot. Luckily, it wasn't. Not yet.

Tess ran in. The lower level had only begun to fill with smoke, tendrils creeping along the ceiling. She kept running until she reached the others. Someone grabbed her arm and said, "Thank God. We were just going to look for you," but before Tess could even see who it was, she was swallowed by the rush of girls coming down the stairs and getting into formation.

Tess grabbed younger girls and hurried them to the line. As she did, she kept scanning faces, ticking them off a mental checklist. One was missing—the girl Tess looked for the hardest, the one she feared wouldn't be there. Eleven-year-old Maggie, who devoured novels as fast as Tess did and had started on Tess's own library, which the matron deemed "a little too old" for the younger girl. Tess disagreed—there was nothing truly scandalous in those books. So she'd let Maggie read them on the understanding that she do so in private, which she often did at night, curled up with a flashlight in the closet. Whenever Tess returned from visiting Billy, she'd check that closet and shuttle Maggie off to bed if she'd fallen asleep.

When Tess didn't see Maggie, she bolted up the stairs. The higher she climbed, the thicker the smoke. She remembered what the firefighter had said during their last fire drill, and she pulled her shirt up over her mouth and nose to breathe through it. By the time she reached the top, though, it was like stumbling into a campfire, thick smoke everywhere, heat enveloping her, flames crackling.

She followed that crackling and saw flames. On the ceiling. Licking at it. She glanced back at the stairs.

No. Not yet. Don't panic. Just move.

She ran bent over, mouth and nose covered. She kept her eyes slitted, but it didn't help. The smoke set them stinging and watering, and soon she just closed them and felt her way along the wall.

Second door. She needed the second door.

She passed the first. It seemed to take forever to reach the next one. She fumbled for the knob and—

Her fingers gripped white-hot metal, and she fell back with a yelp. Pain ripped through her hand, and she stood there, shaking it, fighting against the pain, trying to concentrate. A deep breath didn't help. Even through the shirt she tasted smoke, and it made her cough. That cough helped her forget the shock of grabbing the scorching doorknob, and she used her shirttail to cover her hand as she turned it. She could still feel the heat stinging her burned hand, but she managed to get the door open.

She dropped onto all fours then and crawled. That was better; the smoke was light enough at floor level for her to see her way to the closet. Through the crack in the door she could make out the faint glow of Maggie's flashlight, dropped when the girl had fallen asleep.

Tess covered her hand again, rose onto her knees and opened the closet door. The flashlight rolled out. She caught it and then raised it to see Maggie sound asleep, wrapped in a blanket, on the closet floor.

She grabbed Maggie's shoulder and shook her. The girl didn't stir. Tess shook harder, her heart pounding now as she realized something was wrong, horribly wrong.

The smoke. There didn't seem to be much in here, but it had drifted through the cracks in the door. How much had Maggie inhaled? Tess struggled to remember what the firefighter had said about smoke inhalation.

She grabbed Maggie by the shoulders and tried to lift her, but the girl weighed almost as much as she did.

The noise downstairs drowned out her cries for help. There was another noise too. The crackle of fire rising to a roar. When she dared glance up, she wished she hadn't. Flames engulfed the ceiling. Embers rained down, scorching her clothes and her face.

She wrapped her hand in Maggie's nightgown and pulled. The girl barely moved an inch before the cheap fabric tore.

Tess had to wake her up. She had to.

She dropped beside Maggie. As she did, she noticed how still the girl was. Completely still. Tess's hands flew to Maggie's chest, but she didn't feel anything.

She wasn't breathing. Dear Lord, Maggie wasn't breathing.

CPR.

Did she even remember how to do it? It was a new way of helping people who'd stopped breathing, and during a first-aid class earlier that year, the older girls had been shown a training film on it. But Tess'd had a bad night before the lesson—a really bad one—and she'd half-dozed as soon as the lights went out.

Didn't matter. She had to try.

Tess tugged Maggie by the legs to get her out of the closet. Sparks flew everywhere. The smoke was nearly impenetrable now, even at floor level. *Get Maggie breathing quickly, or neither of you will get out alive.*

Clear the airway. She remembered that. She tilted back the younger girl's head and opened her mouth and—

Maggie's eyes flew open. "Wha—what?" The girl scrambled to sit up. "Tess? What's…?"

Maggie saw the fire and her eyes went round, and she started to scream. Tess slapped a hand over the girl's mouth and said, "You're okay. Everyone's okay. Just follow me."

It took a moment for the shock to pass. A moment of Tess shaking Maggie and telling her to focus, just focus. Finally, understanding flickered in the girl's eyes. Maggie nodded, and they set out, making their way back downstairs to join the others outside.

Two

EVERYONE WAS FINE. That was the main thing. And that's what Tess kept telling herself as she sat on damp grass, away from the others, and stared at the house. Sitting on damp grass, just like this morning with Billy in the park. Except now fire-hose water soaked the ground instead of dew, and the red-and-orange horizon wasn't dawn—it was the remnants of the house, still smoldering.

The house. Her home.

The girls liked to complain about how much they hated it, but as orphanages went, it was probably a good one. She'd certainly seen kids in town who seemed to have it tougher, with dirty clothes and bruised arms and a look in their eyes that said there were nights when they dreamed of being orphans.

The orphanage might feel like a cage some days, but it was still her home. Now, in the pile of smoking, sodden rubble, she couldn't even tell where her bed had been.

As for the clothing she'd labored over, struggling to make it fashionable despite the matron's rules? Gone. Her box of patterns and reams of cloth and her little wooden box of treasures: fancy buttons and beads and metallic thread? Gone. Her books were gone too. Tales of wild adventure and faraway places. And with them gone, it felt as if her dreams had burned to cinder.

"You still have this," said a voice behind her.

Billy lowered himself to her side and passed over a box filled with carefully rolled bills. Everything she'd earned running errands or sewing for ladies in town. She'd never spent a penny, no matter how tempting. Every bolt of cloth she used had been donated to the Home. Every treasure in her box had been found. Money was freedom, and she'd squirreled away all she had and given it for safekeeping to the person she trusted most.

She had Miss Webster—the home economics teacher— to thank for her foresight in keeping her money out of the house. Miss Webster had once warned some of them not to leave money lying around, because it might prove too great a temptation to any girl who wanted to run away. It had been years before Tess realized the girl Miss Webster meant was her. She wasn't sure which was more offensive, the suggestion that she'd steal from the other girls or that she'd be foolish enough to leave a decent home for street life.

"Can you keep it a little longer?" she asked.

"Of course."

He took the box back. Then he laid his hand on hers and sque ~ed it. She noticed a few of the girls looking over at them, a couple with curiosity, others envy. Lucky Tess, with her boyfriend.

Just a friend, she thought, but that's exactly what I need.

Tess got along with the other girls. She even considered most of them friends. But she felt no real compulsion to seek them out now, knowing they'd get enough support and comfort from others. She'd always kept herself at a bit of a distance. Get too close, and they might discover her secret.

She'd learned her lesson about that. The only person who knew her secret was Billy. He could be trusted with it, perhaps because he had his own.

Secrets that made them different. Secrets that others wouldn't understand. Secrets they both feared might mean they'd spend the rest of their lives hiding what they were.

It was not long before Tess saw Mrs. Hazelton. They'd been summoned to her cottage. The reason—she could barely process the reason. Every time she'd heard someone say it, she'd asked, *Are you certain? Is that really what she said? There must be some mistake.*

But there wasn't. The Home was closing down immediately. It'd been struggling for years, and this was the final straw. No money to rebuild. Homes would be found for the Little Ones as quickly as possible.

Tess was not one of them.

There would be no home for Tess—not an orphanage or a family taking her in. She was too old. And so she was to receive, more than a year early, her dream of freedom. No longer a girl in an orphanage, but a young woman about to walk into the wide world and make her way there.

First, though, there was one last thing: a private conference at Mrs. Hazelton's cottage. That's where she was now, seated in Mrs. Hazelton's study, taking tea with her. As if she was a young woman already. An adult already, come to visit and chat. Only this chat was no idle bit of gossip. It was more. So much more.

"You have something for me?" Tess said as soon as she took her tea. "A clue from my past?"

"How are you doing, Therese?" the matron asked. "I'm sure it's difficult for you, losing your clothing and your books."

A gentle reminder that Tess could be a little blunt, lacking in the social niceties that facilitate normal conversation. A waste of time, Tess thought. But she acknowledged the matron with a nod and a murmured, "And you, ma'am? How are you managing?"

A smile rearranged the wrinkles in the old woman's face. "I'm doing as well as can be expected. Now, about this clue. That's really all it is. I know nothing of your family, Therese. You'd been dropped off at another home by a woman who claimed only to be a friend of your mother's. That home was full, so you were brought here, which means I never even met the woman who left you. All I have of your past is this."

She handed Tess a small cardboard box. Tess turned it over in her hands.

"I know you love your mystery stories, my dear, but you'll find no clues on that box. It is only one that I provided for the purpose. What was given to me is inside. Each of you seven older girls has something from your past. This is yours. Would you like to open it here or...?"

She didn't even wait for an answer, just looked at Tess's expression and said, "Take it outside then, and open it in private. You may return if you have questions."

ℰℯ⌁

Tess took her box out behind the church. Had the other girls opened the secrets from their past with Mrs. Hazelton? Or with one another? Shown them off? Compared them? She had no idea. Right now her heart thumped so loud that they could have been squealing with glee and she'd never have heard them.

Answers. That's what this box held.

And the question? That seemed obvious. *Who am I?* But for Tess, that almost felt incidental. The bigger answer would come when she discovered where she came from, *who* she came from.

All her life, she'd listened to the other girls playing Who Am I?

I'm a foreign princess, locked away here to keep me safe until I'm eighteen.

I'm the child of international spies, who feared for my life and will come for me when it's safe.

I'm an alien, beamed down to Earth until my eighteenth birthday, when my programming will trigger and I'll take over the world, mwa-ha-ha.

Admittedly, that last one was Tess's. It made the other girls laugh and tell her she was crazy.

Crazy.

Even thinking that made her stomach clench. A word shouldn't have such power. She'd tried to rob it of that power by courting it. She'd do and say outrageous things, and the other girls would call her crazy, and she'd be fine with it, because it wasn't the bad kind of madness. The kind she feared. The kind that nudged at her when she awoke from her dreams. The kind that dug its claws into her back when she saw...what she saw.

That was the answer she wanted. Why did she have the dreams? Why did she have the...rest? Where did they come from? Did they make her crazy? *Would* they make her crazy eventually?

She clutched the box tighter. Forget that for now. Forget answers. There was something else in here she craved almost as much.

Adventure.

The box would not contain anything as prosaic as a name. She'd read enough books to know that. If someone, her mother, perhaps—even thinking the word made her heart beat faster. No, a mother was too much to hope for.

Someone then. If someone had a name to give her, it would come in an envelope.

A box meant a clue. The beginning of an adventure. It would be a key to an old train-station locker. Or a lock of hair, tied with a special ribbon only sold in one place. Or a wedding ring engraved with initials and a date. A clue that would set her on the path. To answers. To adventure.

She smiled, and by the time she got the lid off, that smile had turned to a grin.

Answers and an adventure. What more could she want?

Inside was a faded pink satin pouch. One that could easily hold a key or hair or a ring. She felt the pouch. Something within crinkled. She prodded and rubbed at it. More crinkling.

Tess undid the ribbon, reached in and pulled out a folded piece of paper. On it was...

An address and a phone number.

That was almost as disappointing as a name.

She shook herself sharply. Disappointing? It was an *address*. And a *phone number*. A direct link to her past. Did she really want it to be more difficult?

She swallowed. Yes, perhaps she did. She wanted to *earn* her answers. To set off on an adventure and prove herself worthy of them, like the characters in her books. Except most of those bold adventurers were boys. Maybe this was how the universe worked for girls.

No, girls might have a tougher time striking out on adventures, but it certainly could be done, and it was foolish to think that the universe conspired to keep them safely ensconced in their little homes and towns.

She smoothed out the paper with the phone number and address. It threatened to crack at the lines where it had been folded. Old paper. Fourteen years old now. Probably fifteen, actually. She'd come to the Home when she was just over two. Some girls who'd arrived at that age still had memories of their childhood. Tess did not. Just dreams. Dreams she prayed had nothing to do with her former life.

She didn't recognize the area code of the phone number. Her gaze traveled to the address: *16532 Rue Montcalm, Sainte-Suzanne, Quebec.*

Quebec? They'd had a French teacher who'd sworn Tess was French because of her dark hair and dark eyes and Therese as her full name. Mrs. Hazelton had told Tess not to pay her any mind, but ever since Tess had given particular attention to her French lessons and made sure she got the best marks in class.

If this was her home address, then she really was French. A French Canadian. Even thinking that made her feel a little more whole, a little more real. Not just an orphan girl, but a *French* orphan girl from *Quebec.* When you knew nothing about yourself, every scrap that said "this is who I am" was enormous. And here, with this address and this phone number, Tess might have more than a scrap. Much more.

She tucked the note back into the pouch and ran off to find the matron.

Mrs. Hazelton was a popular person today. Tess impatiently waited to see her again.

"I got a phone number," Tess said as she walked in. "And an address."

"I suppose you want to try it?"

Tess nodded.

Mrs. Hazelton pushed the phone toward her. "I'd offer, but I'm sure you'd like to do the honors. You need to dial 1 first, for long distance."

The matron knew it wouldn't be local then? Tess supposed Mrs. Hazelton had always known a little more than she'd let on. That wasn't cruelty—it was understanding that those scraps of identity, however treasured, were like finding a single coin from a buried treasure. One coin seemed like a fortune...until you realized how many more there were, and then suddenly you weren't satisfied with one anymore, and eventually you might even wish you'd never found it, because it only made you greedy for more.

Before Tess could start dialing, Mrs. Hazelton said, "I should warn you..." Then she trailed off and shook her head. "Go on."

Tess dialed the number. She expected her fingers to shake. They didn't. They turned the dial with calm precision. The answers were near. No need to rush now. Just prepare.

She did hold her breath as the line connected. Then, when it clicked, a cold wave of panic seized her.

What would she say? What was she *supposed* to say? She should have planned—

A voice came on the line, speaking French in a slow, measured tone, easy for Tess to decipher.

"*Quel numéro demandez-vous?*" What number are you calling?

It was the operator. Tess struggled for a response.

"*Je voudrais...le—*"

"*Parlez-vous Anglais?*" Do you speak English?

Tess exhaled with relief. This wasn't the time to test her French.

"I do," she said. "The number I called was…" She rattled it off.

The operator had her repeat it and then said, "That number is no longer in service."

"Is there a, uh, forwarding number?"

"We do not do that, mademoiselle. Do you have a name and address?"

"An address."

"I will require a name as well."

Tess hesitated. She'd been about to give her surname— Stacy—when she remembered it wasn't hers at all but a name the matron had given her.

"Just a moment," Tess said. Then she remembered to add, "Please." She covered the receiver. "They need a name with the address. If it's someone from my family, my real name would help."

Mrs. Hazelton's blue eyes clouded with sympathy. "I don't know it. Here, let me speak to her." She took the phone and slid into her "outside" voice—the one she used with tradespeople and such. "This is Mrs. Agnes Hazelton, matron of the Benevolent Home for Necessitous Girls in Hope, Ontario. The young woman you were speaking to is one of our wards. She has a phone number and address that may provide some insight into her family history. Is there anything you can do for her?"

A short pause, then the matron gave the number and address. Another pause. Then, "I see," and "Yes," and "Of course," and "No, I understand." With the last one, something inside Tess crumpled. Her knees threatened to crumple as well, and she had to put her hand on the desk to keep steady. Mrs. Hazelton thanked the operator with a sincere *"Merci beaucoup"* and hung up.

"She couldn't help, could she?" Tess said.

"I was going to warn you that the number might not work. It's been almost fifteen years, Therese. Perhaps I ought to have said something, but..." She shook her head. "The operator did check the address. It's a small town, so it wasn't difficult. There isn't a telephone number listed for it. That's not unusual, she said. It's rural Quebec, north of Montreal. Not everyone has a telephone. As for the number, she could only tell me that it's been disconnected. There's no way of knowing if it was attached to that house beforehand or if it's passed through a few since. The important thing, then, is the address."

Tess looked down at the black lines swimming on the paper; her eyes had misted without her realizing it.

"You think I should…I should go there?"

To Quebec. Take the train to Montreal. Hope to Toronto to Montreal—Tess knew the route, had dreamed of riding it someday.

An adventure. She was about to get her adventure.

And what did she feel? Terror. Bubbling up from that part of her that thought, Me? I'm only sixteen. I've never even been to Toronto, and now I'll go to Quebec on my own? Find this house on my own?

Even as that panicked voice inside her said the words, she felt something else. A slow, delicious thrill—half fear and half excitement.

She was almost seventeen. Old enough to travel in the world by herself. There were girls younger than her in town who'd quit school and gone down to Toronto to become hairdressers or nannies.

"I think you're ready, Therese," the matron said with a small smile. "Don't you?"

Tess nodded.

ॶ

Thanks to the fire, there wasn't much to pack.

Thanks to the fire.

She would never be grateful for the total destruction of her home and belongings, but mingled with her grief was an odd sense of lightness. Of freedom. Terrifying freedom, setting out with little more than the proverbial clothes on her back. But perhaps, in some ways, that made it easier. All her life, she'd dreamed of the day she would head off to Toronto. No disrespect—or lack of love—toward Mrs. Hazelton and the other girls. There would be tearful farewells, but she'd still take the first train out of Hope.

Now that day was here, and she couldn't help but wonder, if it had simply been her eighteenth birthday, would she have gotten on that train? Eventually, yes. But perhaps not immediately. Without something spurring her on, she might have found reasons to linger a few days. This was her home. This was her family. It could not be cheerfully thrown off like a winter coat on the first day of spring.

But with the address, she had a purpose. A reason to leave. And with the fire, she had no reason to stay. She had only one change of donated clothing to stuff into a donated bag, and she would discard both as soon as she could. As charity offerings went, these came from the bottom of the barrel—or a smelly storage bin. Ten years out of date, a couple of sizes too big, hanging off her tiny frame. To call them "well-worn" allowed them a courtesy they did not deserve.

No matter. She was going to *Montreal*. There was no more fashionable place in the country, perhaps on the continent. She was a French girl now, and she would dress like a French girl. Miniskirt and knee-high boots were only a day's train ride away.

Three

TESS WAS GOING to Montreal. Yes, it was only a
stopover, but that was where her train journey would end.
In the city of a hundred bell towers, as Mark Twain had
called it. That's how she'd always pictured it: a metropolis of
soaring towers and sonorous bells.

Billy leaned over as they waited for the train. "You
look as if you'd travel the whole way with your nose out the
window, like our dog heading to the beach."

She grinned. "I would, but I don't think the train
windows open."

He gave her a brief, fierce hug. "I won't say I'll miss you
or this will become a very sappy goodbye. But I'm going to
give you this." He pressed a ten-dollar bill into her hand.

"I don't need—"

"I know. You have almost $140 from the matron and
another $200 from your savings. You could buy an old car

with that. That $10 is to be used for one purpose: phoning me. Yes, we agreed mail was cheaper, and I'll still expect letters, but I want calls too, and if I've given you money for that, you'll feel honor-bound to use it."

"Letters would be fine," she said. "The postmistress will see them, and you know what a gossip she is. As long as I'm writing, she'll tell everyone we're still together."

He gave her a stern look. "That's the *last* thing on my mind, Tess. I want you to call because I want to talk to you. *You'll* want to talk too, but you hate spending money."

"All right." She folded the bill and put it in a special compartment in her donated purse. "I'll phone every third day."

"Starting at the train station in Montreal."

She smiled. "Yes, sir."

"Hold on." He walked back to his parents' Ford Fairlane. When he returned, he was pulling a bright-purple suitcase.

"It was Suze's. She outgrew purple." He set the suitcase on its side and opened it. Inside was some carefully packed clothing. "She outgrew all this too, so Mom told me to give it to you. It's not exactly the height of fashion…"

"It's perfect." She threw her arms around his neck and whispered, "Thank you."

When she pulled back, he was blushing. The other people on the station platform smiled at them. The train whistle sounded, and when she squinted against the sun, she could see the train rumbling down the tracks.

"There's one more thing," Billy said. "Your birthday present. I hope I'll see you again before that, but you can use them now."

He dug to the bottom of the case and pulled out a pair of boots. They were black vinyl, knee high, with low heels and a zipper up the back. Tess let out a shriek.

Billy laughed. "I don't think I've ever heard you do that. Good choice?"

"The best. Oh my god." She caught a couple of less-indulgent looks from adults nearby and amended it to, "Oh my gosh."

"I picked them up in Toronto last month. I hope they fit."

Tess was already out of her Oxfords and pulling the boots on. They did fit. Well enough anyway. She gave him another hug as the train pulled into the station.

"You'll call," he said.

"And write."

"And come back," he said. "Not to stay." He met her gaze. "I don't ever expect you to stay, Tess. But I wouldn't want to think I won't see you again."

"You will. Promise." One last hug, with a peck on the cheek, and he helped her stuff the few belongings she needed into her new suitcase. Then he took the donated bag with the donated clothing and whispered a promise to make it disappear. One last hug, and she was off, climbing the steps onto the train, purple suitcase in tow, trying hard not to stumble in her new boots.

It was a relatively short trip to Toronto, or so other people on the train said. Short for experienced travelers. Long for those who'd never been more than twenty minutes out of town. Endless for a girl straining for her first sight of a big city.

Perhaps it *wasn't* actually her first sight. She might have been this way before, as a toddler on her way to Hope. Maybe she'd spent time in Montreal. She might have even lived there.

Exciting thoughts. Confusing thoughts. She was used to them, though, that disconcerting feeling that came with knowing you'd lived another life, one you couldn't remember. Almost like being reincarnated. *I used to be someone else. Live somewhere else. Answer to a different name.*

She wouldn't think of that right now. She'd think of Toronto. Of two hours to venture from the train station and see the city before making her connection to Montreal. Billy had said the station was right downtown, near lots of things to see and do. He'd suggested she might want to shop, but he'd been joking. She was frugal enough to restrict herself to window-shopping…at least, until she reached Montreal.

When the train finally arrived in Toronto, there was a moment, standing in the cavernous station, when a cowardly little part of her whispered that maybe she should just find the departure gate and wait. She squelched the voice with one squeak of her new boots, turning sharply and marching to the front doors, walking out into…

She would say she walked out into sunshine, and she did, but what she saw first were the buildings. Soaring buildings everywhere. They should have blocked the sun, but somehow it still shone, warming the endless pavement.

She'd never seen so much pavement. That's all there was, no matter which direction she looked. Pavement rolling out like gray grass. Buildings so high she had to crane her neck to see them. And the smells. That was, perhaps, the most shocking part of all. The city *stunk*—of exhaust fumes and baking asphalt and the faintest whiff of smoked meat. Perfume too. So much perfume, bathing her in a cloud of it each time the train-station doors opened and travelers poured out. Tess supposed the smell of it all should make her stomach churn. Instead, it set her pulse racing.

As she turned, she caught sight of one person who didn't fit the scene. He was dressed oddly, in an old-fashioned vest, and his shirtsleeves rolled up, with a red bandanna around his neck and a flat, shapeless hat on his head. More jarring than his outfit was the fact that he walked in the middle of the road with cars whipping past him, his head bent, as oblivious to the vehicles as they were to him.

A ghost. No, please. Not here. Not now.

"Can I help you, miss?"

Tess spun. A man in a porter's uniform stood behind her, holding the door for an elderly woman.

"You look lost, miss," he said. "Can I help?"

Tess didn't glance back at the man in the road. Not today. There would be none of that today.

She looked at the porter and said, "Do you know where I could get lunch, sir? Before my next train?"

"You shouldn't go far, miss. If you want something simple, there's a deli just down the road. If you want fancy..." He motioned across the road, to a grand hotel that sprawled down the whole block. It was the tallest building around, with a beautiful glassed-in roof garden. He lowered his voice. "The tearoom has sandwiches. It's a proper place for a young lady. Very safe."

She thanked him and considered her options. Most days, she'd go with simple and inexpensive. Today though...Tess clutched her luggage handle and started across the road.

Today was special. Nothing—not even the sight of the ghostly man—would ruin it.

Tess ate too much for lunch. She'd expected to have only a sandwich and a glass of water, but when the waitress sat her at a table alone, an elderly couple insisted she join them. When they discovered it was her first time in Toronto, they declared she must have tea. She wanted to protest that she was rather hungry and would prefer an actual meal, but she recalled enough of Mrs. Hazelton's teachings to know she ought not to contradict the elderly. That's when she discovered that "tea" here was the kind she'd read about in novels, with tiny sandwiches and scones and cakes. As she ate, she made a mental note to tell Billy that there were clearly opportunities for bakers in Toronto.

Half of the three-tiered tray was enough to make her stomach bulge. She also drank an entire pot of tea, which was rich and dark and spicy, not like her usual tea at all. Her hosts insisted she pack the rest of the meal for her train trip, which meant she got a dinner as well. In return, they got a story. Some might call it a lie; Tess preferred *story*.

She knew better than to tell them where she was really going and why—if they didn't want her eating alone, her plans would have scandalized them. So she crafted a pleasant tale of a girl from Hope off to see her auntie in Montreal. There were many embellishments. What good was a story if it did not entertain? They seemed entertained, and that, Tess decided, was a proper exchange for the meal. They even insisted on walking her back to the train station and helping her find her gate. She took their address, promised them a postcard from Montreal and said a sincere thank-you and farewell. Then she was off on the next leg of her journey.

The problem with the large meal was that it made her sleepy. The problem with the pot of tea was that it made her jittery. After about two hours the exhaustion took over. Tess fell asleep.

Perhaps it was the rich food. Perhaps it was lingering jitters from the tea. Whatever the cause, she tumbled headlong into nightmares. Dark dreams of dark places. Nightmares of being trapped in rooms so tiny she could touch all four walls without moving, and she kicked and screamed and banged and knew it wouldn't help, that no one would come.

It's for your own good.

That's what the voice said in the dream. It's what it always said. She'd had this dream for as long as she could remember, and it never changed. Trapped in a room too small to even turn around in. Screaming and pounding to no avail, a voice calmly telling her to stop, that she was only hurting herself, that this was for the best, that it was the only way.

Then the room flipped onto its side, and she thumped down, flat on her back. She kicked and screamed harder, clawing wood, slivers digging under her nails, hot blood trickling down her hands and dripping onto her face. She screamed until she was hoarse, and still she kept screaming.

I'll be good. I'm fixed. I swear I am. Please, please, please…

That was when she heard something hitting the top of the imprisoning box. Something raining down, lightly at first, then harder, thumping against the wood.

Dirt. Shovelfuls of dirt.

She'd had the dream so often that she should have known this was coming. Should have known from the start where she was. Not in a room. Not in a box. Not an ordinary one anyway.

Yet to her sleeping self, it always felt like the first time, fresh in its horror. The confusion of the tiny room. The panic as it tipped over. Terror filling her. Then the dirt. And with the dirt, understanding. The sudden truth of where she was and what was happening.

In a coffin.

Being buried alive.

Four

TESS AWOKE WITH a start, then had a second
one as she realized she was leaning on the shoulder of her
seatmate.

"Oh, I'm sorry!" she said, scrambling upright.

The man did not answer or even turn her way. He just
continued talking to the woman seated across from her.

Woman seated *across* from her?

When Tess fell asleep, there had been no row facing hers.

She took another look at the woman. And at the child
sitting directly in front of Tess, swinging his legs against the
seat. The woman wore a fancy dress, like something for a
garden party. The boy was about five, dressed in a little suit
coat with a bow tie and shorts. Not an outfit a child would
wear. Not these days.

Tess pressed her palms to her eyes. *Go away. Just go away.*
When she opened them, the family was still there, the boy
whining that the trip was taking so long.

"You can't see me, can you?" she said.

"Mama!" he wailed. "Answer me!"

"I'm talking to your father, dear. Now hush."

"I'll answer you," Tess said, but she knew he wouldn't respond. They never did. Unlike the man in Toronto, these ones weren't ghosts. She seemed like the phantom. In their world. In their time. Which wasn't possible, but that was exactly what it was like, as if she'd passed through into another period and all she could do was watch until—

They disappeared. Just like that. Quite literally, in the blink of an eye. They vanished, and Tess was back in her regular seat, with no one beside her, her hands clutching the armrests so tightly her fingers ached.

What's happening to me?

It was a question so old she didn't know why she bothered to ask it anymore. It wasn't as if the skies would part and a voice would boom the answer. And if it did...

You're going crazy.

Tess jumped as if she'd actually heard the voice. She hadn't. It wasn't that kind of crazy. The voice was her own, deep inside her, giving the only plausible explanation.

Billy swore it *was* ghosts. The fact that she rarely saw ones like the man in Toronto—old-fashioned figures in *her* world— but mostly seemed to step into *theirs* didn't matter to him.

"It can still be ghosts," he said. "Not just ghost people, but ghost houses and ghost cars." *And now ghost trains.*

Tess knew that wasn't the answer. She could touch the people in other worlds, like the man whose shoulder she'd ested on. Yet she couldn't communicate with them, and if they were really ghosts, wouldn't that be the point of her seeing them? For them to speak to her? Convey an urgent message for the living?

She thought of the man she'd seen outside the train station. The man she'd known, by his clothing, was one of her visions. He'd made no attempt to speak to her. He hadn't even noticed her. So why did she see him?

Tess and Billy had read every book they could find on ghosts, even a special one he'd ordered from Toronto. Nothing in them had supported his theory. That didn't mean he'd give it up though. Tess wasn't crazy. She was just special. Nothing would change his mind about that. And she loved him for it, even if she knew he was wrong.

Billy was the only one who knew her secret. When she was nine, she'd made the mistake of getting caught talking to someone who wasn't there. She could tell they were visions if their clothing was different enough, but other times it wasn't so obvious. She'd been downstairs in the Home and seen a young woman when they were expecting a new music teacher. Tess went over to introduce herself. Another girl had been there. Nancy. Two years older than Tess and as mean as a snake. It didn't help that Tess had gone after Nancy a few weeks before, when she caught her bullying one of the little girls. They'd both been punished—violence was never the solution, the matron said—but Nancy had still wanted revenge, which she'd gotten when she caught Tess talking to a woman who wasn't there.

It hadn't been as bad as it could have been. Tess had denied that it happened, and most of the girls had believed her. She'd hated lying to save herself, but not as much as she hated the odd looks she got from some girls for months afterward. Even that, she supposed, wasn't terrible. They were just looks. It wasn't as if they called her crazy.

It still *felt* like crazy. That was the thing. For as long as she could remember, she'd seen the phantom people and slipped into their world, yet even as a little girl she'd never told anyone, because she knew it was wrong and she knew she must never tell anyone. She knew that as well as she knew her name. More, even, because her name wasn't necessarily her own.

This was her secret. Her burden. Her crazy.

Tess had plans for when the train arrived in Montreal. She would shop. Briefly, of course, but the train would arrive close to dinnertime, and she had no idea how long it would take to get to Sainte-Suzanne, only that the map said it was about fifty miles north of Montreal. She couldn't make it there that day.

Billy's mother knew someone who had recommended a Montreal hotel near the train station—inexpensive but safe. That meant Tess would have time to shop. She would spend the princely sum of twenty dollars on new clothing. No more. No less either. This was her treat to herself.

She'd even written a list on the train. It included underthings. Grown-up ones. Perhaps even with lace. Mrs. Hazelton would be scandalized by that even more than her new boots. The old woman seemed to think that buying fancy underthings meant you planned to show them to someone. Which was ridiculous. It didn't matter if no one else saw them. Tess would, and they'd make her feel grown-up and pretty.

Yes, there were better things to be than pretty, and Tess wanted all of them. Smart, talented, adventurous, witty... But adding pretty to the list was just fine as long as there *was* a list and it wasn't at the top. And it wasn't as if she aspired to be beautiful, which she knew was out of her reach— her nose and chin were too sharp, and her eyes too big. But pretty was a reasonable and attainable goal.

So she'd had a shopping list. After seeing the family on the train, though, fashion was the last thing on her mind. She wandered out of the station and along the surrounding roads. There were shops, but none enticed her, and finally she forced herself to peruse the goods on the carts along the roadway.

Still nothing caught her attention. It was mostly jewelry, and she was not particularly drawn to baubles. Then she saw some bright scarves fluttering in the breeze, and they were like butterflies on an overcast day, welcome flashes of color in the gloom. When she touched one, the young cart owner snapped at her, words coming like machine-gun bullets, too fast for Tess to decipher, but the meaning was clear enough.

Don't touch. Tess hesitated, feeling the gray cloud threaten again, but she pulled herself upright, murmured a polite *"Excusez-moi"* and settled for eyeing the scarves.

She found the one she wanted quickly enough. It was blue and yellow, the dyes entwining and mingling like watercolors in the fabric, which she was certain was silk. She reached out, not touching it, and said, *"Puis-je?"* May I? The woman took in the cut of Tess's clothes, then her boots and suitcase. It was the latter two that seemed to satisfy her, and she nodded curtly.

It was indeed silk. Not cheap imitation goods for tourists, but a true dyed-silk scarf, the kind she'd dreamed of owning. The price? Seven dollars. Tess tried not to gasp. It was worth it—she knew that. Yet that had to be almost as much as Billy would have paid for her boots.

She could bargain. One of the girls in the Home had been to Toronto and explained that with street carts, one was expected to dicker, as if it was an Arabian market.

"Cinq dollars," she said. Five dollars, which was perfectly reasonable as a starting point.

The woman peered at her as if she were speaking Swahili. *"Je ne comprends pas."* I do not understand.

"Cinq dollars," Tess repeated carefully.

"Je ne comprends pas."

There was no way the woman could fail to understand two simple and easily pronounced words. It was a game, Tess realized, with a flash of annoyance.

"Cinq dollars, cinquante cents."

"*Je ne parle pas Anglais.*" I do not speak English.

"*Je parle Français,*" Tess replied. I speak French.

The woman rolled her eyes in dispute and then launched into a volley of rapid-fire French, ending in a question that Tess couldn't possibly answer, because she'd not understood a word the woman said. That, she realized, was the point. Mocking her. *You do not really speak French, little girl.*

"*Six dollars.*" While the pronunciation was slightly different, it meant the same in either language, which should have simplified matters, but the woman still feigned noncomprehension.

A hand reached over and snatched up the scarf. Tess staggered back a step to see a man there. He was old, at least sixty, with wild white hair and a cane. He didn't even look her way, just said something in quick French to the woman. She nodded. Cash was exchanged. Six dollars cash.

The man took the scarf. Then he turned to Tess. "*Six dollars, c'est bien ça?*"

"*Oui,*" she said tentatively.

She reached into her wallet and pulled out a five and a one. They exchanged money for the scarf. The man gave her a twist of a smile. "Welcome to Montreal, mademoiselle."

"*Merci beaucoup.*"

A slight bow. "*Je vous en prie.*" You're welcome.

He nodded, then turned to the young woman and lit into her, his tone saying he was less than pleased with the welcome she'd given a young visitor to Montreal. Tess tucked the scarf deep into her cheap handbag and hurried off.

Five

TESS DECIDED TO leave Montreal that evening. She regretted it almost immediately, but even then she did not turn around. A foolish and impulsive decision. An uncharacteristic decision. When the dark mood descended, though, she would do almost anything to wriggle out from under it.

At the Home, she could bury herself in schoolwork or books or sewing. If the darkness was particularly smothering, she'd grab a bicycle from the shed and ride as fast and as far as she could, until she'd left that cloud behind and could collapse, exhausted, in a patch of grass and stare up at the sky and dream of freedom.

Here, there were no books or needles or bicycles. There was only the open road, her goal at its end. To go to the hotel would mean lying in an empty room, with nothing to do but wait for visions and nightmares. Foolish or not, she had hit the road, and she would stay on it, even if that meant tramping along at midnight.

She'd taken an electric trolley bus across the city. That had been interesting enough to temporarily lighten her mood. The streetcars were gone from Montreal. She'd heard someone on the train talking about a subway, but that wasn't due to open for a couple of years. So they had buses and yellow trolley buses running on endless wires. She'd taken one of them and then transferred to a regional bus, which the Montreal bus-terminal clerk said would take her near Sainte-Suzanne.

To Tess *near* meant "within walking distance," and she was generous with her interpretation of that because she had no aversion to walking. It was only seven in the evening when she got off the bus, with nearly three hours of light left.

"Sainte-Suzanne?" The bus-depot clerk switched to English as soon as Tess unthinkingly greeted her with *Good evening*. "It is nearly fifteen miles, miss. They should have told you that in Montreal."

"Is there another bus?"

The woman shook her head. "No, you will need to take a..." She searched for a word. "Hired car?"

"Taxi?"

The word was the same in French or English, and the woman laughed. "Yes, a taxi. There is one in town, but it is not operating tonight. You can stay at the inn until morning." The woman gave directions. Tess thanked her and left.

Tess took one look at the inn—a grand Victorian that made Tess envision herself standing at the desk, counting out twice as much money as she had paid for her scarf—and decided to push on.

She would hitch a ride. It wasn't the safest way to travel, but she'd read several magazine articles by people who'd crossed the entire country that way. From them, she'd learned simple rules. Smile. Keep walking—you'll look lazy if you stand still with your thumb out. Target older vehicles—they're more likely to stop. If you're a young woman alone, look for women and families, and if it has to be a man, make sure he's old.

Before she left town, she called Billy. She'd forgotten to do that in Montreal, too wrapped up in her gloom. Now she found a pay phone, put in her dime and added more for the long distance. They kept the call short—mostly just a check-in. She kept it light too, telling him about the gorgeous silk scarf and the elderly couple who had bought her tea and skipping the rest, including the part about the hitchhiking, because she knew he'd tell her to splurge on the inn and the taxi, and maybe he was right, but she just wanted to get where she was going.

She used her new scarf to tie her hair in a ponytail. The bright splash of color would make it easier for drivers to see her. More than that, *she* could see the end draped over her shoulder, fluttering in the evening breeze, and it lifted her spirits.

She was in Quebec. She was wearing new boots and a new scarf, and she was going to be a new girl. A new Tess. One with a past and answers. Yes, she knew it wasn't going to be that easy. She wouldn't walk up to this address and find loving parents who'd lost her in a marketplace fifteen years ago and had been searching for her ever since. Those were the dreams of orphans—that they were really only misplaced children. Which was never the case, but it was better than admitting their parents were dead or, worse, had abandoned them.

Still, the answers would be at that house, buried, waiting for a determined girl to ferret them out. And Tess was nothing if not determined.

The universe decided to reward her resolve, and the first car that came along stopped. It was a woman with two little ones. Tess sat in the back and amused the older child—a toddler who took great interest in her scarf. The woman spoke only French, but they managed enough of a conversation for Tess to understand that the woman could only drive her five miles before she needed to turn off. Her husband expected her home by eight, and they were already late. Tess took the ride with gratitude, and soon was walking on the road again, waiting for the next.

She swore she'd walked five miles before another car stopped. A truck this time—a gray-haired man driving a pickup with mud on the fenders and hay stacked in the back.

"Sainte-Suzanne?" she said.

"*Oui.*"

She presumed either he could take her there or that he was heading in that direction. She wasn't certain of the right words to ask for clarification. It seemed that being at the top of her class in French did not mean she was actually equipped to carry on proper conversations here. The accent and inflections were different than what she'd learned. Some of the words too. So she settled for a quick "*Merci*" and hopped in.

When the man said something in quick French, she made the dreaded admission. "*Je ne parle pas très bien Français.*" I do not speak French very well.

The man grinned, and she realized he wasn't as old as he'd looked. Prematurely gray. Maybe only in his late thirties.

"That's good," he said. "Because I don't speak it very well either. Lived here half my life, and I'm told my accent is atrocious. I was saying you can toss your suitcase in the back if you like, but it's kinda dirty."

"I'm fine. Thank you."

He pulled away from the side of the road. "Sainte-Suzanne, huh? You're not taking that au pair job for the Chastains, are you?"

"No, sir."

"Good, because the kids are brats." He winked her way. "And it's John, not sir. Please. So you have family in town?"

She considered her lie carefully. If there was no bus service to Sainte-Suzanne, it wasn't very big, and the fact that this man knew about a local job suggested he was from the area.

"I'm traveling," she said. "My family comes from the region originally, and I wanted to see it."

His brow creased. "On your own? What are you? Sixteen?"

"Eighteen."

"You don't look eighteen. Your folks know you're here?"

"They're...not around anymore."

"Oh."

They drove at least a mile in silence. Then he said, "So you're camping? I can't imagine a tent fitting in that little bag."

Tess cursed herself. She should have come up with a better story. Or taken the taxi in the morning, when no one would ask where she planned to stay the night.

"I'll be fine," she said. Then added, "Thank you."

"There aren't hotels in town, miss. Nearest one is ten miles back."

"I'll go back to it. Or find a place."

"Well, that's just silly," he said. "I've got a spare room. You can stay with me. Us, I mean. My wife and me."

There was no ring on his finger. That didn't mean he wasn't married, but something about the way he'd quickly corrected himself said he wasn't.

"That's very kind," she said. "But I'll be fine."

He shrugged. "Suit yourself."

They drove another few miles. When he turned onto a dirt road, Tess's heart revved again.

"Is this the way?" she said.

She expected him to say yes or that it was a shortcut. In other words, to lie. But he shook his head. "I'm not taking you to Sainte-Suzanne at this hour. It's almost dark. You'll stay with me."

She shook her head vehemently, her scarf and ponytail whipping. "No, sir. Please. Just take me—"

"Stop that." He glared at her. "I'm not some dirty old man. I'm being a Good Samaritan. Your family wouldn't want you wandering around out here on your own."

"Just take me back to the main road. Please. You're right. I should have come out tomorrow. I'll catch a lift back and stay in the inn."

"No, you'll stay with me."

His hands gripped the wheel and, jaw set, he punched down the accelerator. She knew this wasn't a misunderstanding.

She dropped her head and let out a sob. "P-please, sir. Let me go."

He lifted his foot off the accelerator and leaned over. "Hey there. Don't cry. I'm not going to hurt you. I've got a spare bed, and I just want to help. I'll drive you to town in the morning—"

She threw open the door—one hand pushing it wide, the other clutching her purse. The man let out a cry of surprise and hit the brakes, and she flung herself out the door.

It was, in retrospect, a very foolish thing to do. It had seemed clever enough at the time. Trick him with the fake crying so he'd slow down enough for her to jump out. She'd read the scene in adventure stories—the plucky hero escaping from the villain by leaping from a moving vehicle, rolling gracefully into the ditch and racing off.

It did not work like that.

Perhaps part of the problem was that she'd taken the suitcase with her. She'd considered leaving it—while she'd feel guilty abandoning the clothing Billy had given her, no guilt was worth risking her life for. But it was wedged between her legs. If she went, it had to go too. So she flung herself—suitcase and all—out the door and, perhaps not surprisingly, did not land in a graceful roll.

Tess hit the road so hard that for a second she thought, I'm dead. There seemed no way it could be otherwise. The air whooshed from her lungs, and pain ripped through her as she skidded over the gravel, her entire body on fire.

Then she stopped. She lay there, suitcase flung aside as she'd jumped, her arms and legs pulled into an awkward cannonball, as if she'd instinctively rolled up when she hit the ground.

As she vaulted to her feet, pain screamed through her again, and she thought, What if I've broken my neck? She hadn't. Her vault, though, was more of a staggering, stumbling, rocking push to her feet, teeth gritted against the pain searing through her hip and left arm, which were studded with gravel. That's when she heard the slam of the truck door.

She spun to see the man jogging around the vehicle. His face was livid.

"What kind of crazy stunt?" he shouted.

Tess didn't hear the rest. She grabbed her suitcase and ran into the long grass.

"Get back here!" he shouted. "You need to see a doctor!"

She called back that she was fine, still hoping she was being paranoid, that he really had just been trying to help and she'd read too many scary novels, and he'd see she was okay and back off. He did not. He ran after her, shouting that she needed a doctor, that he wasn't going to let her run away when she was injured.

He wasn't going to let her escape. That's what he meant. He'd keep telling her—and maybe himself—that he was doing the right thing. But the right thing would be to see she was terrified and leave her alone. He didn't.

She ran for a strip of trees about fifty feet from the road. When she reached it, she realized how thick the forest was, no path to be seen, and she stumbled and knocked about, struggling to carry the suitcase.

She threw it aside. That was all she could do. Throw it and send up a silent apology to Billy. At least she'd stashed all her money in her purse.

The man didn't stop for the suitcase. He stayed right on her trail, maybe thirty feet back. Branches lashed her as she ran. They whipped against her skinned arm, and she bit her lip against the pain. Her hip throbbed. One knee hurt. It didn't matter. She had to run as fast and as far as she could.

She stumbled a few times over fallen branches and thick undergrowth. He seemed to be gaining ground. That's when she heard a cry and spun to see him going down, arms flailing as he fell. He howled in pain. Tess kept running.

"My leg!" he shouted after her. "I think I broke my leg!"

She slowed and turned. She couldn't see him now; he was lost in the undergrowth. She listened for the heaves of panting breath, the sounds of pain. None came. Silence. Then, "Oww. My leg—I think I broke it."

When she didn't answer, he said, "You wouldn't leave me here, would you? I'm hurt."

No, he wasn't. She was certain of that. Well, at least 75 percent certain.

"Your truck is that way," she said. "Start crawling."

"You little bitch!" He leaped up and she started to run, but his fall must not have been faked, because she heard an honest hiss of pain and looked back to see him holding a tree for support, wincing.

She kept running, and this time she did not look back. Nor did he follow. He shouted after her. Called her an ungrateful brat. And worse. He *was* hurt. Not as bad as he'd faked but enough that he couldn't give chase. That didn't mean Tess stopped running. Not until she burst from the forest, her sides aching, lungs burning. She looked around. The dirt road was to her right. To her left, more trees. She headed for them.

Six

SHOULD SHE CONTINUE on to the address? Did she dare? The question looped through Tess's head as she trudged through the forest. The fact that she was trudging in the direction of the town suggested she'd already made up her mind. The operator had said it was a rural address, and since she hadn't given it to the man—John, if that was his real name—there was no chance he'd be waiting there. She would stay off the roads and keep her eyes open. It was nine now, dusk. Cars had their headlights on and were easy to spot even from these woods.

The terrain here was wild—a few farmers' fields but mostly open meadows and grassy hills and forest patches. That made it easier. She found the main road and continued alongside it, sticking to the long grass and trees.

While she could see the town lit up against the coming night, she wanted to find Rue Montcalm. So each time the main road branched off, she had to scoot close enough to see the sign and then dart back. It was slow going, and the slower it went, the darker it got. Soon she'd passed the turnoff for the village and begun to consider the very real possibility that Rue Montcalm didn't cross the main road at all. As she was about to reevaluate her plan, she saw the name on the next sign.

Rue Montcalm ended at the main road. There was only one way to go, which made it easier. What made it tougher was that it was now too dark to see house numbers unless she walked on the road. She'd be careful and keep her ears open for the sound of a truck.

The road had driveways only every few hundred feet. Unencumbered by the suitcase, she broke into a jog and watched the numbers count down. Finally, she reached 16532. It was not a house but merely a sign at the end of a dark lane. Beyond that, a wooded hill rose sharply. Between the road and the hill, piles of rubble dotted a weed-choked meadow. Remnants of a demolished house.

Tess stared at the rubble. Her eyes burned, and her legs quivered with sudden exhaustion. She imagined her knees giving way, her dropping to them, falling forward and sobbing. Just sobbing. She imagined it, and then she locked her knees, balled her fists and strode up the dirt lane to the rubble-strewn lawn.

Tess picked her way through the grass and brambles and found…a couch. Half of one, at least. Sawed in two, the stuffing gray and stringy. Beside it was something plastic, too dirt-streaked to make out without closer examination, which she did not care to give it. After another few steps, she reached the rubble. It was clearly a pile from a construction site but only a few wheelbarrows' worth. The area was otherwise flat and whole. No sign of a foundation. Not a torn-down house, then, but simply a spot used as a dump by someone too lazy to drive to a real one.

Tess looked over her shoulder at the lane and saw that the drive didn't really end at the forest. A wrought iron gate emerged from the shadowy trees.

She walked to the gate. Beyond it, the lane continued up the hill, and in the distance, atop that hill...

Tess gripped the ironwork to rise up onto her tiptoes for a better look. As soon as her fingers touched the black metal, she gasped and jumped back. It was ice cold. She shivered and rubbed her hands on her thighs. When she touched the gate again, it just felt cool, not surprising given the shade and the plummeting temperature. She peered into the shadows, her gaze traveling up the hill to see...

A house. The top of one, at least. The roof of a massive stone house with spires and columns. The stonework looked yellow—a sickly, glowing yellow. Tess stepped back quickly, rubbing her hands as if the gate had turned cold again. Ice slid down her spine, making her shake, goose bumps speckling her arms.

Run.

That's what her gut said. It saw the house and it said, *Run.* Not a scream. Not a shout. Only a whisper, as if it dared not speak louder.

Quiet. Always be quiet. He'll hear us if we aren't quiet.

Tess rubbed hard at the goose bumps. The chill threatened to turn to panic, and she felt walls closing in, heard the patter of dirt against wood, felt her breath come short, and then she was gasping for breath, the air thin, oxygen evaporating, dirt raining down—

"Stop!"

She said the word aloud. It echoed in the emptiness. She shook herself and grasped the metal gate again, clasping it hard, focusing on the solidity of it, grounding herself. She looked up the hill again and saw just a house. Huge and forbidding, but that's all. The rest was her imagination tearing off down dark alleys, still spooked and unsettled by her encounter with the man.

The gate was chained shut, but it wasn't attached to a fence. Not meant to block the entire property then—just to keep vehicles from going up the lane. She walked around it and started the hike up the hill.

Seven

AS SOON AS Tess crested the hill, she knew why she'd wanted to run from this house. *Foreboding.* That was the word she'd used. Now she had a new one: *terrifying.*

The house squatted atop the hill like a stone troll. A porch stretched across the front, yet it wasn't the sort where you'd sit in a rocking chair with a lemonade in summer. It was cold stone, ground level, with thin columns and no railings. Parapets lined the roofs of the porch, the house, and a carport at the side. The doors looked much too small for the massive building, and the windows, while arched and leaded, were tiny and scarce.

You're not welcome here. That's what the house said. A stone fortress against the outside world.

Go away.

Tess looked up, shivering, at that house, like something from a gothic nightmare, and thought, No.

She would not go away. This address was hers. *Hers.* She had every right to be here, and a mere building would not frighten her off.

She banged the front knocker. The boom echoed as if she'd knocked on the door of Dracula's castle itself. Dead leaves rustled across the porch. Dirt crusted every surface. The forest reached almost to the porch itself. Desolate.

When the wind picked up, Tess struggled not to shiver again. She pulled off the scarf, ran her fingers through her hair and retied it. She wished she could wash her face. After that tumble from the truck—and the hell-bent run through the forest—she could only imagine what she looked like.

She pulled herself up straighter and banged the knocker again.

Still no one answered.

Tess put her ear to the door. Silence. She walked to a narrow window, rubbed a spot on the filthy glass and peered inside. A couch. All right. Someone *must* live here.

Then she noticed the debris on the floor—chunks of wood and plaster on one side, a row of beer bottles on the other, several smashed. The couch tilted backward, one leg missing.

The house was empty.

Abandoned.

She walked to the next window. Another spot cleared; another peek inside. More debris and trash and broken furniture.

Not just empty. *Long* empty.

She swallowed and thought of everything she'd gone through. The train ride. The trip up from Montreal. That man in the pickup. For nothing. She'd been given a puzzle, and she hadn't been clever enough to find the answer.

No, she would find the answer. One way or another.

When the front door proved locked, she tried a side one. Also locked. Then she walked around the back to see a huge fallen branch leaning against a window. Its leaves almost hid a broken pane of glass, the frame swept clean of jagged edges. Clearly a well-used entrance point, probably by the kids who'd left the beer bottles.

She heaved the branch aside and found a flashlight on the ground. Likely left by the kids for their next foray. She put it into her purse and crawled through the window.

Inside, she retrieved the flashlight and shone it around. There wasn't much to see. Rotten and broken furniture. Some trash—mostly Coke bottles and apple cores. A discarded blanket in the corner and the faint smell of smoke told her someone had lit a fire in the huge stone fireplace recently. She could make out shoe prints in the dust.

The room looked like a library, with floor-to-ceiling shelves along one wall. Empty shelves. She bristled as she spotted part of a charred book cover near the fireplace. Books for tinder? Someone had made a pile of the pieces, as if trying to rescue them. When Tess craned her neck, she could see the shelves weren't entirely empty—the higher ones still had books. There was a ladder—an old-fashioned one that ran on rails, like she'd read about in books. It had been shoved off to the far side, and the vandals must not have noticed it.

Tess started for the ladder and then stopped short. The floorboard she was about to walk on had rotted, and there was a small hole, as if an intruder's foot had gone clear through. Tess shone the flashlight around. Nearby boards were warped, threatening to buckle at any provocation. She gave the spot a wide berth.

Tess tugged on the ladder. It squealed like nails on a blackboard, but it moved easily. She positioned it under one of the shelves, climbed up and shone her flashlight on the spine of a very old book. *A Practical Account of General Paralysis.* She pulled down another one that looked so old she expected it to fall apart in her hand. *A Treatise On Nervous Exhaustion (Neurasthenia): Its Symptoms, Nature, Sequences, Treatment.* Nervous exhaustion? She'd heard the term before, whispered in town when the mechanic's wife had a breakdown and had to be sent to the hospital.

No, not to "the hospital." To the Lakeshore Asylum.

Tess shoved the book back onto the shelf hard enough to make the ladder creak. She climbed up two more rungs, until she was at the top row, and took down another book. She saw the author's name first. William Battie. Then the title: *A Treatise on Madness.*

Tess jerked back. The book tumbled from her fingers. She grabbed for it, and her boot slipped. She started to fall but caught herself, her foot coming down hard on the rung below. Too hard. A snap as the old wood gave way.

Tess scrambled for a hold, but she knocked the ladder instead, sending it whizzing along the rails without her. As she fell, she tried to twist, to flip, to do anything to avoid landing on her back.

She hit the floor with a sickening crunch, as if every bone in her body had snapped. Only she kept falling. She felt the impact and heard the crash and the crunch and the snap, and she kept falling.

Falling through the floor. Through the rotted boards.

All four limbs shot out, desperate to catch something, anything, but it was too late. The floor had broken, and she'd crashed through.

Her head struck something, pain lashing through her for one split second before everything went dark.

Eight

TESS WOKE TO complete darkness. Her arms shot out, heart pounding, certain she would flail against the sides of a wooden box and hear the skitter of dirt. But when she leaped up, nothing stopped her. Nothing except a screaming pain in her head that forced her to her knees as she doubled over, heaving and gagging. She lifted one hand to her head and gingerly prodded a rising bump.

Knocked out. She'd been knocked out and thrown into...

She inhaled the stink of mustiness and felt the dirt beneath her fingers.

A basement. She'd been knocked unconscious and thrown into a basement.

There'd been a man. She remembered running though the woods, trees lashing at her, vines catching her feet. Then a cry. A fall.

She'd fallen? No...She squeezed her eyes shut and focused on the memory. *He'd* fallen. Then she'd escaped, and there'd been a house.

A house...

A house and a broken window and a ladder. Books. Falling. Rotted floor.

No one had thrown her in the basement. She'd fallen.

Tess exhaled so suddenly that her stomach heaved again. She gagged. Then she sat back on her haunches and kept breathing deeply, getting her bearings.

Not kidnapped. Not knocked out. Well, yes, knocked out, but only by her own stupidity. All she had to do was find the stairs and get back to the main floor.

She needed the flashlight. And her purse. The first, though, would help find the second, so she searched on the dirt floor. The flashlight was light gray, which should have made it easier to find than the dark purse, but she spotted the bag first, lying in a heap not far from where she'd fallen. She took it and blinked hard, trying to see better. A little light seeped through the hole in the floor overhead. Very little, given that it was only moonlight shining through the library windows.

Tess looked up at the hole...and saw the flashlight teetering on the edge.

She took a deep breath. No matter. She could fix this.

Tess felt around on the floor and picked up a chunk of fallen wood. She positioned herself under the hole and pitched the wood up at the flashlight. Her aim was perfect. The wood hit the flashlight...and knocked it backward out of sight.

Tess responded with every swear word she knew. While she was certain Mrs. Hazelton would disagree, there seemed a time and a place for profanity. A purpose too. It certainly made her feel better.

She squared her shoulders and marched forward...only to stumble over a piece of debris. All right then. Less confidence, more caution. She walked slowly, each foot sweeping the way before touching down. She kept her hands outstretched too, and after no more than five steps she felt concrete. A wall. *See, that was easy.* All she had to do was walk—carefully—along the wall until her fingers found the door.

She was at the first corner when she heard scratching. She froze. Silence. She lifted a foot. Another scratch, long and deliberate. Then another. Tess's mind fell back into that nightmare place, trapped in the box, oxygen almost gone, her fingers bloody and raw, the final slow scratches against the wooden—

She shook herself hard. It was a rat. Maybe even just a mouse, but she would accept the possibility of rats. She'd helped Billy when a few got into the storage shed where his parents kept their flour. One swift kick had sent them scattering so Billy could lay out the traps. Rats, she'd realized, were much more frightening in fiction than in reality.

She tilted her head and listened to the scratching. It came from the other side of the wall. *Good enough.*

Forewarned was forearmed. *Just find the door. Find the stairs. Get out.*

As she felt her way along the next wall, the scratching stopped. A sob echoed through the room. Every hair on Tess's body shot up, and she strained to hear, telling herself she'd misheard, she *must* have misheard...

Another sob, so clear now that it sounded as if it came from directly behind her. She wheeled, turning her back to the wall. A sniffle. Then crying. Quiet, muffled crying. From the very room where she stood.

"H-hello?"

No one replied. Did she expect an answer? Did she *want* one? No. For the first time in her life, she heard a voice in the dark and prayed it *was* her imagination. Her madness. Because the alternative...

"*Aidez-moi.*" Help me.

*No. No, no, no...*Tess rubbed her arms as hard as she could. Pain blazed when she touched her skinned elbow, but she didn't care.

"*Aidez-moi,*" the voice whispered. "*S'il vous plaît.*" Help me, please.

Tess wasn't alone down here, and if she wasn't alone, then that meant...

She thought of the branch covering the broken window. Of the flashlight stored there. Of the blanket and pop bottles inside. Of the smell of smoke from the fireplace, and the footprints, all from one set of shoes. It wasn't a group of kids having a bonfire. It was one person.

A man living above. A woman down here.

Every lurid article from every lurid magazine that Tess wasn't supposed to read flooded back to her now. Tales of women held hostage by crazed killers. Those stories always frightened her more than any monster novel, because monsters weren't real. Not the ones with fur and fangs. Human monsters? They were real, and she'd only needed to read a couple of these stories to know they were not her idea of entertainment.

Was it the man from the truck? Surely two men in the same village could not be kidnapping women. Somehow, in escaping him, she'd come straight to his lair. She had no idea how that was possible, but there seemed no other explanation.

"Hello?" she said. Then, "*Où êtes-vous?*" Where are you? A silly thing to ask, but she did anyway.

"*Aidez-moi.*"

"I will. Just…say something else." Tess started forward, her feet sweeping again. She repeated the words in French— or as near an approximation to them as she could manage.

"*Aidez-moi.*"

Tess followed the sound of the voice as she told the woman to keep talking.

"*Je suis désolée.*" I am sorry.

The voice came from near floor level, right in front of Tess. She crouched and reached out. The woman started crying again…behind her.

Tess went still. "*Où êtes-vous?*"

Soft crying answered…from her left now.

"*Je suis désolée. Je suis désolée. Je suis désolée.*"

Each time, the voice came from another direction. Tess rose, her eyes wide and heart pounding as she backed up until she hit the wall.

"*Aidez-moi, s'il vous plaît. Je suis désolée.*" Help me, please. I am sorry.

The words repeated from every corner of the room, getting louder each time, until Tess shrank, crouching, with her hands over her ears.

"Not real. Not real. Not real."

The voice stopped. Tess straightened slowly, one hand clutching her purse strap as if she could use it as a weapon.

A weapon against phantasms? Against her imagination? Against madness?

She gritted her teeth and resumed her methodical circuit around the room. When the crying started again, her fingers shook, but she kept going. One wall, two walls, three walls...four? She'd reached the fourth corner, which meant she'd gone all the way around and failed to find a door.

That wasn't possible. Simply wasn't. Not all rooms were quadrilaterals. She kept going. Fifth wall. Sixth? Seventh? No, that couldn't be. Then her foot struck the same board she'd encountered on the third wall, and she realized she was going around a second time.

Four walls. No exit.

Impossible. She moved more slowly now, her hands reaching down for cubbyholes and up for hatches. There would be something. There had to be.

There was not.

No door. No cubby. No hatch.

"*Aidez-moi, s'il vous plaît. Je suis désolée.*"

Tess clapped her hands over her ears. No doors? Fine. There was a hole in the ceiling, wasn't there? And debris below. If she could pile it and climb—

Footsteps sounded on the floor overhead. Slow, heavy footsteps.

Nine

TESS MOVED AWAY from the hole in the ceiling and huddled in the corner farthest from it as she listened to the footfalls.

"*Qui est là?*" a voice said from above. Who's here?

A male voice. Not a child's but not old enough to be the man in the truck.

"*Il y a quelqu'un?*" Is someone there? Then a grunt, as if in disgust, the voice growing stronger now as he said in French, "I *know* someone's here. You took my flashlight. Come out," followed by something she couldn't translate.

The footsteps stopped. A clatter. The flashlight turned on. A curse then. Or she presumed from his tone that it was a curse, though such vocabulary had not been part of their French lessons.

A thump. A dark figure appeared over the hole. He shone the light straight down at first, as if looking for a body. Then he moved it aside, and she saw a boy, her age or a little older.

Straight dark hair fell around his face as he leaned over the edge of the hole. He wore a denim jacket, frayed at the collar and cuffs. In one hand he held the flashlight. In the other...

He moved the beam, and it glinted off a switchblade. Tess shrank back and held her breath, but as soon as he shone that light around the small room...

"*Merde*," he muttered and eased back onto his haunches with a deep, aggrieved sigh. Then he leaned forward again and spoke rapid-fire French. It was clearly a question. When she didn't reply, he said it again, and Tess decided that whatever the situation, cowering wasn't going to help.

She rose and brushed herself off. "Do you speak English?"

"Not if I can help it." His English was thickly accented but much better than her French, so she ignored the sentiment and said, "I fell."

"No kidding." Another grunt, as aggrieved as his sigh, and he pushed to his feet. "Get out of there and find your own place for the night. This one's mine."

"There's no way out."

"Sure there is. It's called a door." He started walking away. Tess hurried over to the hole as he said, "Don't ask for my flashlight either. If you need light..."

He tossed something down. She caught a book of matches.

"Just don't burn the place down," he said. "You've done enough damage."

"You don't understand," she said. "There's no door."

A snort. Boots clomped as he returned to the hole and shone the light down. "It's right—"

The beam passed over four solid walls. Then it crossed them again, slower.

"No door," she said. "If you spot a secret hatch, though, I'll be happy to take it."

She couldn't see his face very well, given the angle and the shadows and the hair falling around it as he leaned down. But when he looked her way, she could see his eyes— gray-blue and narrowed, as if it was her own fault for falling into a doorless room.

"How much to get you out?" he asked.

"What?"

"I thought you said you spoke English."

"I do. I—" She realized he was being sarcastic. "A dollar."

"Two."

"One-fifty."

"Throw it up."

Now it was her turn to snort. Which she did—and tossed up two quarters. "You'll get the rest when I'm out. And only if you throw me the knife first."

"What?"

"The knife. I'm not climbing up there while you're holding a knife."

He scooped up the quarters. "Then I guess you aren't climbing up here."

"Do you want the dollar?"

"Do you want to be rescued?"

"Rescued, yes. Mugged, no."

More eye narrowing. "Do I look like a mugger?"

"You just demanded payment to rescue someone trapped in an abandoned basement."

"Payment for services rendered. Not theft."

Tess could argue that, considering her alternative seemed to be slow death by dehydration, it certainly felt like robbery. But she settled for saying, "Still, you can see where I'd be concerned, being rescued by someone with a knife who seems determined to turn a profit in the matter."

"And you can see where *I'd* be concerned, giving my knife to someone who obviously doesn't think I *deserve* to turn a profit in the matter."

"You think I would—" She paused. "You have a point."

His brows lifted, as if surprised she'd admitted it. He hesitated, then drew back his hand—the one holding the knife. If he'd been a moment slower, she'd have ducked and probably yelped, but fortunately for her ego, he threw it before she realized what was happening. The knife shot to his left and landed with a *thwack*, embedded in the wall.

"There," he said. "Out of both our reaches."

"Thank you."

He grunted and walked away. To find something to haul her up with. Or so she hoped.

☙

Tess stood a reasonable distance from the hole and struggled to catch her breath. He'd located a rope, which sounded like the obvious way to pull someone out of a basement, but again, it hadn't been as easy as it seemed in books. She'd climbed and he'd pulled—less than she climbed, she suspected—and now they were both recuperating from the operation.

He was smaller than he'd seemed looming over that hole. Shorter anyway. Billy was five foot nine and lamenting his chances of reaching six feet. This boy was about the same age but a couple of inches shorter. He was slender and wiry— he'd pulled off his jean jacket for the rescue operation. When she'd first come up over the edge, she'd thought he was Native Canadian, with his straight black hair and light brown skin, but those gray-blue eyes suggested there was more. *Métis* was the word that sprang to mind, courtesy of a history teacher who'd been enamored of the Louis Riel story.

Métis were originally the children of French trappers and Native women. Of course, the days of trapping were long past, but the Métis remained a distinct culture. Whether this boy was Métis or simply of mixed race was irrelevant though. Anything about him beyond the fact that he'd come by at a very good time was irrelevant.

"Thank you," she said, graciously she hoped, as she passed him a dollar bill.

He grunted and pocketed it.

"I'm Therese," she said. "Tess."

He gave her a cool, level stare. "And I'm the guy who had to rescue you. Let's leave it at that. The exit is over there." He pointed at the broken window.

"Can I ask you—"

"No. Whatever it is, the answer is no. I'm tired, and this is my place. Go find your own."

"Can I just ask—"

"Did I say no? Now unless you want to rent a room from me..."

Her expression must have answered for her.

He chuckled. "Thought so. Go away, little girl. You've caused enough trouble tonight."

He went to retrieve his knife, and Tess decided to do as he asked.

Tess spent the night in the forest, as close to the house as possible. Given the alternatives, it seemed safest, which proved exactly how unsafe her life had become since leaving Hope. She was exhausted enough that she barely had time to consider her surroundings before she dropped into as deep a sleep as if she'd been home in her bed.

At dawn she was back in the house, sitting in the least smelly armchair, waiting for the boy to wake up. He finally opened one eye, spied her through a curtain of hair and jumped up, one hand brushing his hair back, the other fumbling for the knife that was, apparently, not where he'd left it. That's when he finally recognized the intruder and started swearing in a creative mix of English and French and possibly a third language.

"You left it over there." She pointed at the blade by the fireplace. "You must have been as tired as I was last night."

"What part of go away wasn't perfectly clear?"

"I went away. Then I came back." She hopped from the chair and walked over. "I have a proposal for you."

"A what?"

"A job. I would like to hire you to—"

He cut her off with a sputtered laugh. "And what makes you think I'm in the market for a job?"

"You demanded money to rescue me last night."

"Maybe I just didn't appreciate the inconvenience."

"You're living in an abandoned house, which means you're a runaway. Unless you're eighteen, which makes you a vagrant instead."

His eyes narrowed. "A vagrant? Why would you say that?"

"One look at you."

More narrowing. "Is that right? So you just presume, based on my looks, that I'm a vagrant."

"Yes. You need a shower. Desperately—"

"What?" He seemed genuinely surprised. Apparently, he hadn't seen a mirror in a while.

"Shower. Water plus soap. Shampoo would be nice. Your T-shirt is dirty and your jeans look like they could stand up on their own."

He said nothing.

"What?" she said. "If you don't believe me, I'm sure there's a mirror—"

"That's what you meant when you said I look like a vagrant?"

"Yes. Your hair is too long, but you don't look like a hippie, which is always another excuse for the lack of showering."

"Uh-huh…"

"If I had to pick—"

"Please do." He crossed his arms.

"I'd say runaway, not vagrant. You don't look eighteen, and even if you were, you're too well educated to be a vagrant. Despite the accent, your English is perfect."

"That's not education. That's growing up with an English mother."

"Which would not explain your level of diction."

His face screwed up. "My what?"

Tess sighed and returned to the chair. "If you wish to pretend you're a tough kid from the wrong side of the tracks, go ahead. I can see the advantages of the ruse if you're living on the streets. But take my advice. Use smaller words."

"You think you're clever, don't you?"

"Not particularly. Better than average perhaps."

He shook his head.

Before he could speak, she continued. "I'm not interested in the specifics of your situation."

"Really? Could have fooled me."

"Have I asked you a single question? No. I simply offered you a job. I *do* have questions about this house, though, which you may or may not be able to answer. If you cannot, I'll ask for your help obtaining them in town, as your French is significantly better than mine. I'll pay you five dollars for a day's work."

He stared at her.

"It's a lot, I know," she said.

"I wasn't thinking that. I was wondering if you're as crazy as you seem."

She tried not to flinch. "Probably. But I have money. So in this case, crazy is to your advantage."

He pushed up from the floor, walked to the fireplace and picked up his knife. Then he took three slow, deliberate steps toward her. "And if I'd prefer the money without the work?"

"I don't have it on me."

He seemed to bristle at that. "Because you expected me to steal it?"

Tess sighed. "You threaten to take my money at knifepoint and then get offended at my suggestion that you're a thief. More advice? If you're going to affect a persona, you have to stick to it."

"I don't know what you're talking about."

"Liar. As I said, your story is none of my concern. I hid my money as a general precaution because I don't know you.

All I have is this." She took the five from her pocket. "You could steal it, but you said last night that you don't steal money. You earn it. I'm offering you the chance to earn it."

"You're crazy."

"I've heard that. So…" She waggled the five. "A fair day's wages."

That familiar narrowing of his eyes. "Half now."

She ripped the bill and handed him half. "So, where do we get breakfast?"

Ten

BREAKFAST COST TESS a dollar, as the boy reasoned she should cover his as well, and she didn't feel like arguing. She did argue, though, when he tried to send her to town for it.

"You don't need to speak French to buy a baguette and jam," he said. "Point and hand them the money."

"My French is fine." She paused and then opted for honesty. "Passable anyway. I just…I can't go to town alone. Last night…" She paused. "I can't. If I'm buying your meal— and paying your wages—you can do it."

She squirmed under his cool stare, more gray than blue. An uncomfortable stare, almost painful, as if he was digging answers from her brain with the tip of his knife.

"All right," he said finally. "But give me another couple of dollars for lunch. I'm not going down there twice."

He grumbled but put his hand out and took the money.

ℓℯ◝

Over breakfast—baguettes and jam and Cokes—Tess told
the boy her story. The pertinent part, that is. That she'd
grown up in an orphanage and knew nothing of her parents
or her background. That the Home had burned down a few
days ago. That she'd been given this address as the key to her
past. The boy listened intently at first. Then he frowned.
By the time she finished, his eyes had gone steel gray.

"Who set you up to this?" he said, barely unhinging
his jaw enough to get the words out, which only made his
accent thicker and he had to repeat himself before she
understood.

"Set me up to...?"

"Someone sent you here with this...story."

"I don't know what—"

"Out!" His voice boomed through the empty house as
he waved at the broken window. When she didn't move,
he threw the partial five-dollar bill at her. "Get out!"

"No."

He took a step toward her. His face flushed dark, jaw
tight, eyes cold. The switchblade stayed in his pocket,
and he made no move to take it out. Which meant he was
serious. He only pulled the knife for show.

Tess crossed her arms. "I'm here to find out where I
come from, and I'm staying whether you help me or not."
She looked up at him. "Whether you *let* me or not."

"Did you forget I have a weapon?"

"No, but I came all this way to get whatever answers this house has. It's my birthright."

He snorted at that.

She straightened. "It is. It's the only thing I have—"

"You gave me some advice? Let me give you some. If you want to tell a sob story, tears help."

"It's not a—"

"It's a lie."

"My matron gave me the box, which she's had since I arrived as a baby—"

"Then *she's* lying."

"She would not."

"One of you is."

Tess got to her feet. The boy eased back a half step, as if she might fly at him. She only gave him a look as cold as his own. "I'm searching this house for clues. If you want the other half of that five, you'll help me. Otherwise, don't get in my way."

$$\mathcal{e}\!\!\frown$$

Tess sat on the floor, surrounded by piles of books. She'd taken every one off the shelves—fourteen in total—and sorted them into piles by subject. Five were medical texts. Three were on mental illness. Two were biographies of people she'd never heard of. Four more were random classics—for entertainment, it seemed.

The whole time she carted down and sorted books, the boy sat on a chair and watched. Now, as she flipped through one of the biographies, he said, "You're serious about this."

She decided the question did not require an answer and kept reading. The book was, apparently, about a psychiatrist who'd worked for the Germans during the war.

"I think someone's lying to you," he said.

"Every girl in the Home got a clue about their past," she said, not looking up from her book. "Something that was left with them when they arrived. Mine had a phone number—which is out of service—and this address."

She made it through three pages before he continued, "I don't know how or why, but you've been set up. This is about me."

"Everything is, I'm sure." She closed the book, keeping her finger in it as a marker. "I'm quite certain I haven't been sent here for the sole purpose of annoying you. No one is that important. Not even you."

He scowled.

"Sorry." She resumed reading. "*C'est la vie.*"

"Is it possible that—"

"No," she said.

"I didn't finish—"

"You don't need to. I'm trying to read. If you're not going to help…" She flicked her fingers. "Go away."

"Excuse me? This is my—"

"Your house?" She lifted her brows at him. "It's your temporary—and illegal—lodging, which I will return to its original condition when I leave. Except for the hole in the floor, of course."

"Are you always like this?"

She turned the page. "Like what?"

"Weird."

She tried not to stiffen. "Yes. I am. And you're defensive, paranoid and, at this moment, irritating. We all have our faults."

Five pages of silence, but she could sense him standing there.

"There's nothing in the books," he said finally.

She glanced up at him.

"I've looked at them," he said. "I was curious about this place. They're textbooks—mostly medicine and psychiatry. What matters isn't the contents but the context. Why they're here. What this place was."

"Was?"

"I think..." He considered and then picked up the ripped five-dollar bill. "I'll show you."

ॐ

"Do you have a name?" Tess asked as the boy led her up a flight of stairs.

"No."

"Let me rephrase that. What's your name, so I have something to call you?"

"Why? There's no one else here. If you're talking, obviously it's to me, right?"

Not necessarily, she thought but let the subject drop. They'd taken a quick tour of the ground floor. He hadn't wanted to bother—growing impatient when she insisted—and she'd quickly seen why. It looked like the ground level of any large house, with a library, several sitting rooms, a dining area and a kitchen. The bathroom, she'd noted with some dismay, was nonfunctioning, which meant she'd have to continue using the forest.

"Are you on the run?" she asked as they reached the top of the steps.

"What?"

"You thought someone sent me after you. You're exceedingly paranoid. That suggests you're in hiding."

He scowled over his shoulder at her. "Or on the run from the law?"

She paused. "I hadn't considered that."

"Yes, you have." He gave her a hard look. "Don't play dumb. Just say it."

"Say what?"

He turned, blocking her path down the hall. "You thought I was a vagrant."

"Because you're dirty."

"Right. And when I went into town this morning, the *boulanger* watched me like I was about to stuff that baguette under my shirt and race off. Then, when I did pay, he checked the bill to make sure it was real. Why's that?"

"Because you're dirty."

He crossed his arms and scowled at her.

"What? You are. You don't smell yet, but I suspect if you don't bathe by tomorrow—"

"Don't be obtuse. It doesn't suit you."

"All right. I *do* think it's because you're dirty, but it might also be because you're a teenage boy. You—"

"Where did you say you're from?"

"Hope, Ontario."

He grunted and shook his head. "Not many people like me in Hope, I take it?"

"Oh, you mean...I was going to say Métis, but not everyone of French and Native Canadian mixed ancestry is Métis, and that's probably rude." She paused. "Is it rude? Not to presume, but to ask?"

"No." He headed down the hall. "It's not rude. Just don't expect me to answer."

She continued after him. "The only reason I thought that at all is because I had a history teacher who was fascinated by Métis culture and history. Especially Louis Riel. I think she might have had a crush on him." She quickened her pace to keep up. "I could call you Louis, if you won't give me a name."

"*That* would be rude."

"No ruder than not giving me a name to use."

"This is the second floor, as you doubtless guessed. Six rooms."

"Bedrooms, yes. I can see. Fascinating."

"You see two bedrooms, which we just passed. Two more are offices. The last two are empty."

"Empty?"

"Empty. *Vide.*" He said a third word—one she couldn't catch—and then, "If you need another language, you're out of luck. Those are the only three I know."

"What's the third one?"

He pushed open a door and waved inside. "As I said."

She peered in. "It's empty."

He muttered something under his breath. Tess was sure it wasn't a compliment. When he'd said the room was empty, though, she'd expected he just meant it didn't contain anything of significance. But this room didn't simply lack furniture. The floor and walls were bare boards. The ceiling had been left intact, but the fixtures were missing.

"That's weird," she said.

"Then we agree on something."

He walked to another door and pushed it open to reveal the same thing.

"So only two people lived here?" she said. "Well, up to four, if it was two couples or a couple and kids, but the house is big enough for twenty."

"It is."

He opened a door at the end of the hall. Stairs extended into darkness. He went first, his flashlight on. It didn't get much brighter at the top. Dirt caked two dormer windows. The walk-up attic had been converted into a third level. Narrow doors lined a narrow hall. Tess walked to one and—

"Locked," she said and started for the next.

"They're all like that," the boy called after her. "I broke open the one at the end."

He stayed at the top of the stairs as she continued on. She pushed the half-open door. If the house looked like something out of a gothic novel, this was a room where the manor lord had kept his mad wife. Smaller than a jail cell, with a metal cot and nothing else. No dresser, no window, no closet. Presumably there had been a mattress on the cot, but even with that Tess couldn't imagine it was comfortable.

She walked to the door.

"It locks from the outside," she called.

"Uh-huh."

"You'd need a key to open it from the hall, but there's no way of locking it or unlocking it from inside the room. It's like—"

She stopped as a loud click sounded. She stepped into the hall to see him opening a door farther down. "I thought you said—"

Her flashlight glinted off a long, thin piece of metal in his hand. A lockpick? She'd seen them in mystery magazines. So he'd gotten his back up when she suggested he might steal something, but he carried lockpicks?

When she stepped into the hall, he pocketed the pick fast and leaned out of the room. "Got this one open. I wanted to see if it was the same. It is."

She headed down and peeked in. "Exactly the same."

"So presumably, we don't need to open the others. This is what we have. Eight locked bedrooms."

"Cells," she said.

He grunted and didn't reply, just headed down the stairs, leaving her to hurry after him. When they got to the bottom, she examined the attic door.

"It has a lock," he said, still walking. "From the outside only."

She followed him down the stairs to the main level and through to the kitchen. He stood in the middle of it and pointed at a floor-to-ceiling cabinet.

"The basement," he said.

He watched her, a little smugly, waiting for her to ask what he meant. She walked to the cabinet, poked her fingers behind it and felt a doorframe.

"It was hidden like this when you found it?"

He covered any disappointment that she'd figured it out. "I discovered it last night, after you fell through. Before that, I figured there wasn't a basement. But that wasn't just a little crawlspace you fell into. So I hunted and found this."

She wedged her fingers in behind and wiggled the cabinet.

"It's nailed in place," he said.

"You didn't get it free?"

"Yes, I went out at midnight, stole a pry bar and half killed myself moving the cabinet, only to put it back afterward."

"So that's a no?"

"If you want it moved, I will help. The key word there is *help*."

"All right. So we need a pry bar?"

"Or some kind of tool. I'm not an expert. There's a hardware store in town."

"Let's go then."

Eleven

"I THOUGHT YOU didn't want to go to town," the boy said as they returned to the house's library.

"Not alone," Tess said. "I'll go with you, but you'll need to do most of the talking. My French is not as good as I thought it was."

"It won't get better if you don't use it."

She nodded. "If we could switch to French sometimes, that will help. Thank you."

A flicker of dismay said this was not what he'd meant, which she knew very well. A low threshold for annoyance, mixed with an equally low quota of patience, meant he'd hardly be the person to help her improve her language skills. But he'd opened the door and she'd sneaked in, and now he was trapped. He might be surly, bordering on rude, but he seemed unable to cross the line and actually be rude.

"It's important to learn French," she said. "My teacher says it might become an official language in Canada someday.

That's what the Royal Commission on Bilingualism and Biculturalism is discussing. She says—"

"I know the politics," he said. "Better than you, I'm sure. If you want to practice on me..." He sounded pained. "Go ahead. Just...I'm not a teacher, and I don't have time to play one. Back to the town visits. I'm not sure having me talk to the locals will help."

"Are they all like the *boulanger*?" she asked.

He hesitated as he reached for a knapsack hidden under his blanket. "No," he allowed. "But it's a small town. French, Catholic and white. They're...standoffish. Part of it's how they'd treat anyone from outside, including you. Part of it's because they don't know how to treat someone who's Métis."

"So you are?"

A grunt as he pulled a comb from his bag. "Cree Métis. Both sides." He turned to hand her his comb, but she was already brushing her hair.

"That must be nice," she said. "Knowing exactly where you come from."

An odd look crossed his face, then he gave a brusque "Yes" and shoved the comb back into his pack.

"Do you have a washcloth in there?" She motioned to his bag. "That might help you with the locals."

He gave her a look. "Yes, I know I could use a shower. They're a little hard to come by out here. But I'm not—"

She handed him her makeup compact. He saw his face in the mirror and let out a curse. Dirt streaked one cheek, and a smear of it crossed his forehead. He pocketed the mirror and, without a word, took a bar of soap from his pack. Then he grabbed a collapsible jug of water from the table and headed outside. Tess followed.

The boy stripped off his jean jacket, leaving his shirt on, and washed his bare arms with soap and water. Then he rubbed his hair between his fingers with another curse, as if only now realizing how badly it needed shampoo. He looked at the water jug, seeming to consider whether he could spare enough. She was about to say they didn't have time for that when he dumped half of it on his head and used the soap to lather it up.

"You should have told me how bad I looked," he said. "*Before* I went into town for breakfast. No wonder the *boulanger* wanted to run me out of his place."

Tess bit her tongue and said only, "Do you have a towel? I can grab it—"

"Don't have one," he said as he rinsed his hair. "You?"

"No."

"You should get your bag anyway. Put it inside. I'm not going to steal any of your clothes—I doubt they're my size. Or color."

"I don't have a bag."

"What?" He swiped his wet hair out of his face and peered at her. "What did you do? Just drop everything and come out here?"

She considered saying yes, that's exactly what she'd done, but she could tell he'd think her an idiot, and perhaps that shouldn't matter, but it did. It always did.

"I brought one. It's just…not here. I had…a problem, and I had to leave it."

His eyes narrowed. "Problem?"

She fussed with the scarf in her hair. "I might be able to get it back later. I'm fine for now. We should get going."

He squeezed out his hair and tugged his jacket back on. They started down the driveway.

"We'll need a story," she said. "Who we are to each other. In case anyone asks."

"None of their business."

"That's not going to encourage them to talk to us."

"I thought we were just going for a pry bar."

"And to ask questions, of course, while we're there. What this place is. Was." She glanced at him. "You seemed to have a theory."

He shrugged.

"You think it has to do with those books."

Another shrug.

"An asylum. That's what you're thinking, isn't it?"

An asylum. For crazy people. That's where her address had led. Not to a home, to a family. To the worst possible answer. That her greatest fear wasn't unfounded. That somehow, she'd come from this. From madness.

"It's called a psychiatric hospital," the boy said, his voice gentler than she'd heard it. "It's for people with mental illnesses. *Illnesses.*"

"Where they lock them in tiny rooms without even a window?"

"For their own safety. And even if it was a psychiatric hospital, that has nothing to do with you or your past. It's a house. Other people have lived there. Probably your family at some point." He seemed to struggle for something nice to say. "It's a fancy house. Your family would have been rich. Important."

She said nothing. He was wrong. Her nightmares and visions couldn't be a coincidence. If anyone in her family had lived here, it wasn't because her family owned the house; it was because someone in that family had been a patient. Whatever illness he or she had, it had been passed on to her, and it was deep in her brain, ticking like a bomb, getting ready to explode and—

"So what's this story you think we need to tell?" he said.

She blinked, reorienting herself. "Cousins."

"What?"

"With a boy and a girl of our age, they'll figure we're dating, and they won't like that, us being on the road together alone. So cousins. I was given the address for the house and told it would answer some questions about my parents, who died when I was little. As my cousin, you're here to help with my language barriers."

He considered, as if looking for holes to poke in her story. Was he disconcerted when he found none? Maybe. He said nothing, though, just kept walking.

She continued. "And since it will no longer be just the two of us, I'll need a name for you. It can be fake."

Silence.

"How about Ringo?" she said.

A hard look. "Don't tell me you're one of *those* girls. The Beatles are coming to Montreal in September, and I'm already planning to be out of the province. I remember when they announced the concert—I swear I heard girls screaming from a mile away."

"The Beatles are all right. I like the Stones better."

His eyebrows arched, as if shocked that a small-town girl knew who the Rolling Stones were.

"I could call you Mick," she said.

"No, you could not." A few more steps. "It's Jackson."

"I need a first name."

A glower. "That *is* my first name."

"So what do you go by? Jack?"

"No."

"Sonny?"

A more emphatic "No." Then: "If my parents had wanted to call me Jack or Sonny, that's what my name would be. It's Jackson."

"Huh. That's different."

"So I've heard."

He walked on quickly, leaving her jogging to catch up.

"It's not French," she said.

"No kidding." A few more steps, then: "I'm named after the painter, if you must know."

"Jackson Pollock?"

Again, he seemed surprised that she knew him. He nodded. "My mother met him when she was a kid, and I guess he made an impression. Good enough? Or are you going to keep interrogating me?"

"It's not interrogation. It's curiosity. And since you seem perfectly fine with ignoring my questions, I feel perfectly fine with asking them."

He sighed, and they continued on.

ℯ⁓

"No one lives there," the woman at the hardware store said. She spoke French as Tess struggled to mentally translate.

"Obvious—" Jackson began irritably before Tess cut him short with a kick. She was beginning to think her broken French might be more useful than having him speak for her.

"You aren't hanging around up there, are you?" the woman asked. "Didn't you see the signs?"

"We only went up to have a look," Jackson lied. "It was *empty and* obvious—" He stopped himself. "And it didn't seem as if anyone lived there. How long has it been empty?"

"Sixteen years."

"What?" Tess interjected in English. Then a quick *"pardonnez-moi"* to the woman and to Jackson, "Can you ask if she's sure? That's before I went to the Home."

Jackson asked. The woman was certain—her sixteen-year-old daughter was born the summer after the last owners left.

"So it's been abandoned for sixteen years?" Jackson asked.

"Empty, not abandoned," the woman said. "It's still owned by someone. There's a caretaker."

"Can we get his address?" Tess cut in, asking in French and adding a heartfelt "*s'il-vous-plaît.*"

"*Oui.*"

ᖶ

Before they left to find the caretaker, Jackson asked the woman what the house had been used for. No one in town knew exactly, she said. All they had figured out was that it had been occupied by a group rather than a family. There had been a barbed-wire fence surrounding the grounds, and locals had been asked, very nicely, not to hunt or otherwise trespass. The man in charge had seemed to be a doctor, and in explaining the need for privacy, he'd mentioned patients. Locals guessed it was some kind of sanatorium or private hospital.

The caretaker turned out to be younger than Tess had expected. Maybe in his early twenties. He worked as the local plumber, having taken over when his father passed on two years ago.

"That's when I took on the house too," he said. "It used to be my dad's responsibility."

"How long did he do it?" Jackson asked.

"Since the folks up there moved out. The doctors or whatever. I was about eight, so…sixteen, seventeen years ago?"

Jackson asked more pointed questions about the type of doctors, but the young man knew nothing more. "There were stories," he said. "Especially about this one guy, who snuck up there on a dare at a bonfire party. He got teased because he was so scared when he came back. But I was little at the time. Maybe six. The kids involved were teenagers. So I don't know what he saw. You'd need to ask him."

He gave them the man's address, and then Jackson asked more about the house and the caretaking responsibilities. As they might have guessed from the look of the place, his job wasn't to keep it in move-in condition. His main task was just enough basic upkeep to avoid violating any laws and having the house condemned. The occasional group of local teens would throw a party there—he admitted to doing that himself when he was younger—but they usually cleaned up afterward and didn't do any damage, so he turned a blind eye.

He also paid the annual taxes. That money was wired to him, as was his monthly stipend. Both came anonymously.

"I don't know the owner's name," he said. "I've never had any contact with him. The deed lists a company in Montreal. I looked it up when I was there once—just curious, you know—but I couldn't find any record of it."

Jackson wrote down the name and address of the man who'd trespassed on a dare, and they headed out again.

Twelve

THE MAN THEY needed to speak to lived outside town. When Jackson turned onto his street, Tess slowed. It was the same dirt road the truck had gone down the night before.

"What's the name of the witness?" she asked.

"Witness?" A short laugh. "You make it sound like—" He caught her look and stopped. "What's wrong?"

"Nothing. I'm just curious."

That appraising gaze again. She must have passed muster, because he resumed walking and said, "Etienne."

French for Steve. Tess exhaled in relief. While she suspected the man in the truck wasn't really named John, she recalled him saying he'd lived in Ontario for half of his life, which meant he'd go by Steve, not Etienne. If she was to estimate his age, she'd say he was close to forty, meaning he was too old to be the high-school student the young caretaker remembered. Still, she couldn't help casting anxious glances at the farmhouses they passed, half expecting "John" to appear out of one. Having Jackson there would help. John was unlikely to bother her if she wasn't alone.

They reached the address. And there, in the drive, was the pickup truck.

If someone had asked Tess before if she'd recognize the vehicle, she'd have said no. She recalled only that it was gray. Or silver. Or maybe even light blue. Now, seeing it again, there was no doubt. This was the truck she'd escaped from the night before.

Tess backed up behind the hedge that concealed the house from view.

"Can you handle this?" she asked.

"What?" Jackson hadn't seemed to notice her stopping. His expression suggested he'd been deep in thought.

"I..." She struggled for an excuse. Should she warn him? She didn't know enough about men like John to be sure. It seemed he'd gone after her because she was a girl, not because he'd wanted to rob her—the farmhouse was big and in good repair. The Etienne they were looking for probably wasn't even John but someone else who lived here. And they *did* need to speak to this Etienne. He was their only witness, however much Jackson scoffed at the word.

"I think you should handle this by yourself," she said carefully. "He might not want to discuss it, and we really need to know what he saw at the house, and you're...better at making people talk."

He nodded, as if she'd paid him a compliment, then added, "My dad's a lawyer."

"Good. So you know how to get information from reluctant..."

"Witnesses?" His lips quirked in what might have been a smile.

"Yes. If you go at him hard, I might be tempted to interfere, like I did in town. It'll work better if it's just you."

"All right."

"Can you get him outside?" she asked. "So I can listen in?"

With that, his usual annoyance returned, his lips tightening. "I'm perfectly capable of remembering and relaying—"

"It doesn't seem safe to go into a stranger's house." Which, in this case, was the truth. Even if she didn't think John posed a threat to a teenage boy, she wanted Jackson outside, where she could watch and intervene if necessary.

When she said that, though, he rolled his eyes. "I'm a guy. I'm almost eighteen. I have a knife."

"Please?"

She expected more eye rolling at that, but to her surprise, he gave her that piercing look and then said, "All right. But only if he comes outside easily."

ℰ◠

Etienne did come out easily. And it *was* John. Or rather Steve, as he told Jackson, laughingly explaining that the locals had changed his name for him to make him properly French. Jackson suggested they switch to English, which Tess mentally thanked him for. It did make it easier to eavesdrop from her hiding place beside the big front porch.

"I'm interested in a house," Jackson said.

Steve laughed. "I'm not a real-estate agent. And you look a little young for home ownership."

"It's the one on the hill. The abandoned one. Well, empty, I'm told. Not abandoned."

"Oh." The ebullience drained from Steve's voice. "You aren't hanging around up there, are you?"

"No, but I'm told you did once. Back when it was still occupied." Jackson wove a quick story about an aunt his mother had lost touch with almost twenty years ago, and the house on Montcalm was the last address they had for her.

"Oh," Steve said again. That was it. *Oh.*

"You went up there on a dare, when you were a teenager..."

"Yeah."

"And you saw..."

"Nothing."

A missed beat before Jackson said, "Nothing?"

"That's right."

When Jackson spoke again, there was a new note in his voice. Authority, as if he really was a lawyer in a courtroom. "I've been told otherwise. You went up to that house and—"

"And I didn't see anything."

"So you got spooked and ran away after seeing *nothing*?"

"I didn't *see* anything. I *heard* something. And whoever said I got spooked and ran away—"

"Irrelevant."

Despite her anxiety at being so close to the man who'd tried to kidnap her, Tess had to laugh at the silence that followed, as Steve undoubtedly wondered whether this kid was a lot older than he looked.

"I'm not interested in what you did," Jackson said. "Only what you saw. Or in this case, heard."

"All right." Steve cleared his throat. "Crying. I heard crying."

The hair on Tess's neck prickled.

"Crying?" Jackson said. "You were frightened off by that?"

"I wasn't—" Steve cut himself short. "It wasn't just crying. It was sobbing and pleading, and then there was screaming. That didn't last long. The screaming, I mean. Lights went on, and then I heard footsteps, as if someone was running to stop it. Then it stopped."

"You heard a woman screaming—"

"A man. The crying was a woman, but the screaming was a man. That's what freaked me out. Hearing a man scream like that? It was awful. I've never heard anything like it before."

"So you heard a woman crying and pleading, and a man screaming, and someone running to silence him…and you returned to the party and didn't tell anyone?"

"I'd been trespassing."

"You heard *screaming*. Like someone was being hurt, and—"

"It was some kind of hospital. People are in pain in a hospital, so there would be crying and screaming. That's normal."

"If it seemed *normal*, it wouldn't have scared you."

"Look, kid, I answered your questions. We're done."

The door banged shut, Steve retreating. Then it creaked open and Steve said, "Hey!" as if Jackson had gone in after him.

"Get the hell out of my—"

"Hold on. What's this?"

"My, uh, daughter's suitcase. Also, none of your business."

"Your daughter's name is Thérèse?"

Tess froze. Billy had rewritten the luggage tag on her suitcase. Steve must have left the suitcase just inside his door.

"Sure. It's a nice name."

"It's also the name of a friend of mine. Who lost her luggage on the way here yesterday."

Staying low to the ground, Tess hurried along the porch to the steps and climbed them silently as Steve gave a sheepish laugh. "All right. You got me. I found it outside my place this morning. I do have a daughter, and she was hoping no one would claim it, because there are some nice clothes inside, and she figured if it was left behind, it was trash, but I've been telling her we need to turn it in at Sainte-Suzanne. If it's your friend's, go ahead and take it and tell her I'm sorry—"

"For what?"

A pause. "Hmm?"

"Sorry for what?"

Another pause, Steve clearly trying to decide how much Jackson knew. "For taking it, of course. She should be more careful with her belongings. I really was going to turn it in. I was just trying to convince my daughter—"

"You don't have a daughter."

"Excuse me?"

"There are two pairs of shoes by the door and three coats on the rack. All men's."

A strained laugh. "What are you, a detective? Get out of here, kid. Take your friend's bag—"

"I'll go as soon as you tell me the truth. Where'd you get the suitcase?"

Tess crept toward the door, her heart pounding.

Drop it, she thought. Please, Jackson. Just drop it.

Of course, he didn't. He might hate answering questions himself, but when he asked them, he expected an answer. He continued to badger Steve until the man said, "I don't know what she told you—"

"That she met some guy," Jackson lied. "And that's how she lost her bag."

"It was a misunderstanding." A whine crept into Steve's voice. "I was trying to be friendly, giving a girl a lift. If you're her friend, you need to teach her not to hitch. It isn't safe."

"Obviously."

"*Hey*. No. I was helping her. Giving her a lift and offering her a place to stay—"

"A place to *stay*?"

"It was just an offer. She freaked out and jumped from the truck. She must have been high on something. She left the bag behind, and I was waiting for her to come down from the drugs and get it. Now take—"

"I will. And I'll get the full story from her. When I do, it better match yours, or I'm going to be back with the police. Is that clear?"

"Get the hell out of my house before I—"

Tess crouched, ready to swing around the corner, but Jackson was already dragging the suitcase, scraping the floor.

"I'll be back," he said. "You'd better still be here."

Jackson walked out, his face hard, eyes blazing. When he saw her, his expression changed. No softening of his features. Just a change in his eyes. From blazing with anger to ice cold, skewering her with an accusing glare. She reached for the bag. He jerked his chin, telling her to get moving, and followed her off the porch.

Thirteen

THEY WALKED DOWN the dirt road in silence. Several times, Tess tried to take the suitcase, but Jackson stopped her with a grunt and kept walking, and she could do nothing but hurry along beside him.

"You lied to me," he said.

"I—"

"What did he do?"

She didn't answer.

"*Thérèse.*" He said her name in the French way—*Tair-ez*—and she flinched. "If you don't tell me, I'm going to have to presume he's right and it was a misunderstanding and you overreacted, and if that's not the truth, then you need to tell—"

"It might be."

"What?"

"It might be the truth. I…I don't know. He didn't say anything weird or try to touch me. He offered me a place to stay, and I said no."

"You said no."

She stiffened. "Of course."

"I'm not questioning that. I'm pointing out that's not *his* story. If you refused and he insisted..." He glanced over. "That's what happened, isn't it? He insisted, and that's why you jumped from the truck without your suitcase."

"I took my suitcase."

"That's not the point."

"I'm just saying I took it. I had to leave it behind. In the woods."

"Because he chased you?"

She nodded.

A hard look. "And you still think it could have been a misunderstanding?"

"I—I guess not. I said no more than once, and he started driving to his place..."

"*Not a misunderstanding.*"

"I don't think it was planned. He was just—"

"Taking advantage of the situation? Getting you to his place so he could figure out his next move?"

She nodded.

"That doesn't make it any better, Tess. Not at all. It's still kidnapping. The moment someone tries to forcibly..." He trailed off and cleared his throat. "The legal definition isn't important. But just because he wasn't grabbing you and telling you what he planned to do doesn't make him any less culpable. You knew something was wrong. Go with your gut. Don't ever worry that you're overreacting."

She nodded.

A flicker of discomfort as silence fell, and he said gruffly, "I have sisters. That's what my parents taught them. Someone should have taught you the same thing."

She nodded again.

"You knew whose house it was, didn't you?" he said after a few minutes of silent walking. "*That's* what you lied about. You let me go up there, knowing—"

"That's why I told you to talk outside. So I could listen."

A humorless quirk of a smile. "And run to my rescue?"

"I know I'm not exactly big and intimidating. But I could have done *something*."

"I appreciate that, and you're right—it would have helped. However, what would have helped me even more was a warning. I'm not accusing you of putting me in danger, Tess. I'm saying that if you want my help, you need to give me more than five bucks. You need to give me some honesty. Otherwise, I'm fumbling in the dark."

"I'm sorry."

He looked over, as if checking that her apology was sincere. It was, and he seemed to see that and nodded.

"That's why you asked me his name, isn't it?" he said. "You saw the road and thought it was him, and the name confirmed it."

"Actually, no. When he picked me up, he said his name was John."

"So he lied about his name, and you still think he might *not* have been planning anything?"

"You're right. The age seemed wrong too. It's hard to tell with the gray hair. It wasn't until I saw the truck that I knew. But I should have told you then."

"Yes, you should have." It wasn't a rebuke. She almost wished it was. This was quiet, thoughtful, and that stung more.

Tess reached into her pocket and pulled out the other half of the five. "Take this. You've done more than enough. I'll get that cupboard moved—"

A snort, sounding more like his usual self. "By yourself? I don't need your mon—" He stopped short. "I'll help you with the cupboard. I'm heading there anyway, obviously. Might as well."

I don't have anything better to do. He didn't say that, but she heard it in his tone. He'd told her to be honest, but that seemed to apply only to her. He'd said he was *almost eighteen,* which meant there wasn't much chance he was a runaway. By that age, he could get a job and find a place to live, and no one would bother him. He said his father was a lawyer, which meant he wasn't poor, despite his rough clothing. Well educated. Well spoken.

The dirt from earlier had been accidental—the result of sleeping in an abandoned house and not having a mirror handy, and as soon as it was pointed out to him, he'd rectified it with his kit of hygiene supplies. Not a vagrant or a runaway then. Finished his last year of high school and hit the road for a summer?

She could ask him if she was right…and she knew the response she'd get. None. She'd have to wait for more clues to this particular puzzle.

ر

It was late afternoon by the time they returned to the house. They got right to work. Jackson grunted that he wasn't hungry and didn't need lunch. She knew he was lying after he spent ten minutes trying to pry off one nail, cursing it in three languages for its stubborn refusal to yield.

"It would help if you did more than supervise," he snapped when Tess defended the poor cabinet.

At the time, she was sweating and straining to pull the cabinet far enough from the wall to allow him to wedge in the pry bar.

"I'm putting all my weight into it," she panted.

"All ninety-five pounds?" he said.

"A hundred and five."

A snort of disbelief, and a shake of his head, as if her size was clearly a personal failing, one designed solely to annoy him.

"You're hungry," she said. "It's making you more irritable than usual."

"Than *usual*? I'm not irritable."

"He says, snapping and glowering."

A scowl her way. "I'm not hungry."

"Liar."

He opened his mouth to retort, but the rumble of his stomach stopped him. He tossed down the pry bar, and it clanked to the floor, making her jump. As he stalked off, she followed, saying, "I know you're curious about what's in there—"

"No, I just want to get this job done so I don't have to share my lodgings again tonight."

"You didn't share them last night."

"I woke up to find a girl in my room. Bad enough."

"Most guys wouldn't think that was so awful."

She said it lightly, teasing him, trying to draw out a smile, but he only glowered at her and then moved faster.

"I was joking," she called after him.

"Good."

"You are curious," she said. When he looked back sharply, her cheeks heated. "About the basement, I mean."

"No, I'm not."

"Liar."

Another scowl, and he picked up his pace. She smiled and hurried after him.

Jackson wolfed down his sandwich. Then he ate half of hers. He'd only take it after she insisted she wasn't very hungry— somewhat true—and that she could eat the bakery goods they'd bought in town—completely true. It was a relatively small sacrifice that bought her some goodwill. She even got a "*Merci*" out of it.

Moreover, when they headed back to work and she continued speaking in French, he didn't insist they switch to English. He did pause, and she could see him considering whether coaching her language skills added another layer of inconvenience to a conversation that seemed inconvenient to him even in English. But he seemed to decide that having eaten half of her lunch, he was beholden to her and should make some small sacrifice of his own. It wasn't long, however, before she was the one regretting the idea.

"*Bon sang! Ça fait mal!*" he said when she accidentally let go of the cabinet, squashed her fingers and said, "Damn it! That hurt!"

"Not funny."

"*Ce n'est pas drôle,*" he translated, then caught her look and said in English, "I'm not mocking you. If you want to speak French, you need to stick to it. Even if your fingers get crushed."

"It's heavy," she said.

"*C'est lourd.* And don't give me that look. If you're going to do something, *fais-le correctement.*" Do it right. "Now, do you *want* to learn French?"

"*Oui.*"

"*Très bien.*" A pause, and then he jerked his chin toward her fingers. "*Est-ce que ça va?*" Are you okay?

"*Oui.*"

Fourteen

IT TOOK OVER an hour to move the cabinet. It seemed
to have been nailed from the opposite side, which was impossible, of course. But they had to wedge the cabinet from the
wall and awkwardly work at each nail. Ten in all. Finally,
they pulled the cabinet away...to reveal a door, nailed shut.

"*Fais une pause*," Tess said. Take a break.

"*Non, ça va.*" No, I'm doing fine.

He wiped the sweat from his forehead; dirt had trickled
down with it, smearing his face. She didn't mention that.
The cabinet was filthy, and she must look just as bad. He'd
been the one doing the prying, though, and while he might
be in good shape, his lean biceps quivered from the exertion.

"*Tu es un bon professeur*," she said, telling him he was a
good teacher to distract him and give him a break whether
he wanted it or not.

He only grunted in answer. She was beginning to learn
that the grunts and snorts were a vocabulary all their own,

equally translatable. This one wasn't derisive but acknowledged the praise with mild discomfort, a boy who'd rather skip the niceties of polite conversation, even when they flattered him.

"You said you're almost eighteen," she said in French.

He replied with a nod and eyed the nails on the door, as if coming up with a plan of attack while also taking a moment to catch his breath.

"Are you still in school?" she asked. "I don't know how it works in Quebec."

"Junior matriculation is grade eleven. Senior is grade twelve." He switched to English for that, but she still had no idea what he meant.

"Junior..."

"Matriculation. It means you can graduate from high school then, but if you want to go to university, you take the extra year. Senior matriculation."

"So you're done school," she said, switching back to French. "Are you going to uni—"

"We need to move this cabinet farther. Give me more room."

And that was the end of the conversation. As long as it stuck to the general, he was fine. Personal? That was none of her business.

They spent another hour working on the door. Finally, the nails were out. Jackson swung it open, and they peered down into darkness.

"Shit," he said.

"*Merde?*"

A hard look. Then. "*Oui. Merde.* The lesson ends here. We have more important things to worry about."

"*Je vois.*" She cleared her throat. "Sorry. I mean, I see."

Despite the darkness below, they could both see enough to know that they were *not* seeing something very important: stairs. The basement door opened into yawning darkness. Tess walked to the edge and put her foot down. Jackson yanked her back, only to release her arm so fast she nearly *did* tumble through the open doorway.

"I wasn't actually stepping down," she said. "I was checking."

He picked up the flashlight and shone it through the doorway. "There. Better? No stairs."

She moved forward, and he rocked on his heels, as if refraining from grabbing her again.

"I'm not stupid," she said. "I won't fall through."

"Says the girl who already did so less than twenty-four hours ago."

"But I can see *this* hole."

"And it draws you, like a magnet, to repeat the experience. If you fall through again, I'm not rescuing you."

"Of course you are. The alternative is to let me die, and I don't think you want to be rid of me *that* badly."

He muttered something under his breath.

"I'm fine," she said. "I'm just looking…" She peered into the basement, lit by the flashlight beam. "No ladder either.

It's a straight drop. Maybe ten feet? Twelve? About the same as the room I fell into. We can use that rope to get down."

She expected him to laugh. Call her crazy. Refuse to help. But he walked a step closer, keeping his distance from the open doorway, as if she might shove him through. He angled the light down and said, "We can try." Then, without another word, he went to get the rope.

They tied the rope around the cabinet, which, Jackson pointed out, was not only heavy but wouldn't fit through the doorway, making it a safe anchor. He insisted on going down first and then made sure he could climb back up, lest they both found themselves trapped in the basement. Curious but cautious.

Jackson lowered himself to the bottom again and let Tess shimmy down. They found themselves in an empty basement room with closed doors on all four sides. Jackson walked to one, turned the knob and put his shoulder against it, as if ready to force it open. As soon as the knob turned, the door opened and he nearly fell through. Tess bit back a laugh and walked past him. He reached out as if to pull her back, then seemed to think better of it and said only, "Careful."

"I know."

This room was also empty…and again, it was a hub for three more doors. Jackson passed her this time, heading for the door on the left. Tess walked to the one straight ahead, threw it open and stepped inside.

Stepped into darkness. Complete darkness, Jackson's flashlight beam already lost in the other room. Her hands shot out instinctively, the old nightmare flashing even as she told herself she was being silly, that her hand would not touch down on—

Wood. It touched on solid wood, right in front of her. Tess spun, hands still out, feeling wooden walls on either side. A box. She was trapped in—

"*Thérèse*," Jackson said. He said something more, about wandering off, but Tess didn't catch it. All she heard was the thundering of blood in her ears as she turned toward the door, and then she saw light and—

The door swung shut. Her foot had been holding it open, and as soon as she turned, it closed and Jackson said, "Tess!"

Her fists crashed down on the door, banging as she screamed and—

The door opened. The flashlight shone in her eyes and she stumbled back, panic filling her, seeing bright light, her gut telling her that was worse, worse than the darkness, worse than—

"Tess!" The light lowered, and Jackson grabbed her arm, steadying her. "It's a closet. The door is on a slant, so it shut by itself."

His lips twitched in a wry smile, as if about to tease her. Then he saw her face and stopped.

"Tess?"

She pushed past him and out into the main room as she gulped air.

"Are you claustrophobic?" he asked.

"Y-yes."

"All right. Put your head down. Take deep breaths. Close your eyes."

She did fine with the instructions...up to the part about closing her eyes. The moment she did, she was back in that room, clawing her way out, air thinning as she—

She opened her eyes and stuck with the deep breathing.

"That's some serious claustrophobia. Have you talked to anyone about it?"

She shook her head vehemently, still bent over.

"You should. My mom's a psychologist and—"

"Wh-what?" She jerked upright. "A psychiatrist?"

"Psychologist. That means she has a PhD. A psychiatrist is a medical doctor. Doctor, doctorate, it's confusing. They're both called doctor, but a psychologist doesn't have medical—"

"I don't need a shrink."

His face tightened. "It's not like that. Therapy is for anyone who has a problem that interferes with normal life—"

"I don't."

"And I'm not saying you do. I was...Never mind. So you found a closet."

"It's *not* a closet."

He sighed. "If you're still upset over the therapy thing, I wasn't recommending—"

"It's not a closet."

She strode over and looked inside. Four walls, enclosing an area of less than ten square feet. It might *look* like a closet, but she knew it wasn't. She took the flashlight to shine it up on the ceiling.

"There's nothing there, Tess," Jackson said.

"Exactly. If it's a closet, where's the rod? Hangers? Hooks? Shelves?"

He went quiet, and she thought he was considering her words, but when she looked at him, he seemed to be struggling to figure out how to phrase something. "If this was a private psych hospital, it wouldn't have rods or hooks in the closet. They present a...danger."

"Of what?"

He searched her gaze and said nothing.

"Of what?" she repeated. "I'm not squeamish, Jackson. Tell me—"

"Suicide."

She flinched. She didn't mean to. The thought of suicide bothered her, of course. There'd been a girl in the Home, a couple of years older than her, who'd tried once, and Tess and another girl had found her. It'd been one of the worst experiences of her life, and maybe that explained why she flinched now, but it seemed more the combination of the two things: a psych hospital plus suicide.

"People who come to a place like this aren't crazy," Jackson said. "Not the way you read in books and see in movies—the wild-eyed nutcase. A lot of them are just depressed. If they're depressed enough, they might try suicide."

"I know. There was a girl, in the Home..." She trailed off.

He nodded. "And I'm sure she wasn't crazy. So the closets wouldn't have rods or hangers, Tess. There would have been a dresser or boxes. Safe storage."

Safe storage. The nightmare flashed again, trapped in a box. Upright, screaming for—

"Tess?"

She snapped out of it. "So this main area is a bedroom?"

"Sure. The ones in the attic would be for patients requiring extra restraint—"

"Restraint?"

A flash of annoyance, his kindness fraying fast. "So they don't harm themselves and, yes, possibly others. Hitting or scratching during an episode. Possibly delusions if it's schizophrenia. People in a private mental hospital aren't crazed killers, and the people keeping them there aren't evil jailers. It's a hospital, not a lunatic asylum."

"I'm sorry."

He deflated a little. "I don't mean to get on you about it. Most people think the way you do. I know better, because of my mom, and it bugs me when people flip out at the mention of mental illness and psychiatric hospitals."

"I'm sorry. I just..." She swallowed. "Too many books, I guess."

A wry twist of a smile. "Nothing wrong with books, even those kind. Just...don't take everything you read at face value. Educate yourself."

"Yes, sir."

He made a face. "That sounded pompous, didn't it? Sorry. Let's keep looking."

Fifteen

THE ROOMS WERE not bedrooms. Even Jackson conceded that after a few minutes. They were too interconnected, with areas that could only be reached by passing through other rooms, which wouldn't work for private patient quarters. There were more "closets" too. One room had two, side by side. Jackson still insisted that whatever the purpose of the larger rooms, someone had clearly constructed these small ones for storage.

Most rooms were empty. A few contained discarded furniture, piled up as if had been moved from elsewhere. There were a couple of old desks too, but riffling through the drawers didn't yield any clues. Then they reached a locked room.

"You can open it, can't you?" Tess asked as Jackson peered at the keyhole.

"It'll take some work." He crouched and said, with deliberate nonchalance, "I don't know about you, but I'm starving.

I have apples in my bag. Would you mind grabbing me one? Take one for yourself too. I'll have this open before you get back."

"I saw the lockpick earlier, Jackson."

She expected him to protest, but he said, "I didn't want to give you the wrong idea. Since you already seemed to have it."

"What idea?"

"That I'm some kind of delinquent."

"It was a first impression. You're living in an abandoned house, carrying a knife, in need of a shower…"

"*That* was a mistake. I didn't realize…" He trailed off and shook his head. "Can we drop the shower jabs? It wasn't *that* bad, and I'm fine now." He rubbed his cheek and then sighed at his dirt-streaked fingers. "The point is that you'd formed an early impression, and seeing me picking locks wasn't going to help. I mentioned that my dad is a lawyer. He has clients with…special skills. When I was a kid, one of them stayed with us for a while and taught me some things."

"How to pick locks?"

"It wasn't like that. He was an activist."

"A what?"

"Activist. Sometimes, to change the world, you need to break a few rules. Or locks. Not my dad's point of view, but his clients can get themselves into trouble. For a good cause."

"Oh." She had no idea what he was talking about.

"One taught me to pick locks. I was ten and wanted to be a detective. Anyway…" He turned to the lock. "Just don't get the wrong idea about me."

"I won't."

He wasn't an expert—it took a fair bit of effort and cursing to unlock the door, but finally he turned the knob. She pushed the door open and brushed past, flashlight in hand.

"Um, Thérèse…" he said.

She shone the light up, and he shielded his eyes. "I don't need a boy to walk into danger ahead of me. I'm quite capable of doing it myself."

"So I've seen. I mean that I think I should be first through since I got it open."

"Oh. You're right. Next time."

She turned, flashlight beam crossing the room as he sighed behind her. When she stopped short, he bashed into her and cursed. Then he saw why she'd stopped, and he cursed again before cutting himself short and saying, "They're for storage, Tess."

Boxes. That's what she saw. Not crates, but long wooden boxes exactly the dimensions of…

"Coffins," she said.

"Caskets," he corrected. "A coffin has six sides, like in the Old West, and we don't use them—" He caught her expression. "Okay. You don't want the etymology lesson. But these aren't caskets or coffins or any container designed to hold dead bodies." He took the flashlight and walked to one. "They're just for storage. Unfortunately shaped boxes."

He lifted the lid on one. It was hinged. Like a casket. Inside, it was just a rough wooden box.

"See?" he said. "Not a casket."

"It looks like—"

"No lining. No padding. *Not* a casket."

"And that?"

She pointed at another box, in the corner, with the lid propped open. Its interior was padded. Jackson strode over and stuck his hand inside, smacking the padding hard as if expecting it to prove an optical illusion.

"It's the wrong sort of padding. Caskets have satin linings. This is vinyl."

"Let me guess. You have an uncle who's a funeral director."

His face darkened. "Of course not. I've been to funerals, and I pay attention. If you're suggesting that I'm lying about my parents' professions—"

"I'm suggesting you don't know as much as you think you do. About a lot of things."

Now his eyes chilled to gray steel. "I know caskets—"

"Then what *is* this?"

He hesitated.

"I'll give you a minute," she said. "That should be enough time for you to come up with an explanation that proves I'm an ignorant little country girl."

"I'm not trying—"

"You do. Whether you mean to or not."

His mouth opened, then closed. He stood there, lips pursed, before saying, "I'm not calling you ignorant, Thérèse. I'm pointing out that these cannot be caskets. It makes no sense."

"Didn't you say that sometimes mental patients commit suicide?"

"By the dozen?" He waved across the room.

"There are four boxes."

"You know what I mean. Yes, occasionally, despite best efforts, a mental patient commits suicide. They're not going to have four caskets in the basement, just in case. Even if they did, for some bizarre reason—maybe they treated suicidal patients and the rate of failure is higher—what are the caskets for? To bury them in the backyard? These people would have families."

"Not everyone does."

He dipped his chin in an unspoken acknowledgment. "True, but even if the hospital had to tend to the arrangements for a patient or two, they wouldn't store the caskets here, Tess. You can't bury bodies in your backyard."

"Not legally," she said. "But if you were trying to hide—"

"No."

"I'm saying—"

"No." Anger crept into his voice now. "That's not the way a mental hospital works. If you're going to say that it was a secret hospital, where people locked up their crazy relatives—"

"Then I've read too many books. Because that never happens. Never, ever, ever." She stepped toward him. "Just because that's not how a hospital is supposed to work, doesn't mean it never does. I read an article a few years ago, by Pierre Berton, about a hospital in Orillia, not far from Hope. It was for the mentally challenged, and it said they were abused and drugged and held down in ice-water baths, and *that* was a legal hospital. The families of those kids were just happy someone else was taking care of them. You can't tell me that couldn't have happened here. That there couldn't be illegal hospitals, if someone was willing to pay enough."

"But these aren't caskets, Tess. They just aren't."

"They're padded, human-sized boxes. What else would they be for?"

"I don't know."

"But you know they absolutely could not possibly be caskets?"

He sunk onto one. "No, I don't."

He sat there, leaning forward, flashlight beam bouncing off the floor and illuminating his face, all sharp angles and shadows, curtained by his hair. He looked lost. A boy who wasn't used to not having answers, lost in uncertainty and indecision, his eyes empty, as if his mind was whirring behind them, consuming all his energy as he searched for answers, digging into the darkest corners of a jam-packed brain but still finding nothing useful.

Tess watched him and felt...She wasn't sure how she felt, only that she wanted to go and sit with him, brush his hair out of his face, tell him it was all right, that he didn't need to have the answers. He'd jump like a scalded cat if she did, and then he'd scowl at her and give her that cold glare, as if by showing a moment's tenderness she'd committed some grievous offense. He didn't want that. Not from her. Maybe not from anyone, but she had a feeling it was mostly her.

She seemed to rub him the wrong way, as the matron used to say about girls who couldn't get along. Their personalities clashed, and there was no getting past that. When Tess looked at Jackson, she wished there was a way past that.

So she settled for taking a slow step toward the box he was sitting on, preparing to lower herself beside him, not too close, not interfering. Just sitting with him. The moment she turned around to sit, though, he pushed up, flashlight rising.

"We should finish looking around," he said. "It'll be night soon."

Which made no difference in a basement without windows. But she knew what he meant. Stop thinking. Start moving. So she did.

Sixteen

THEY DID MANAGE to locate what seemed to be a doorway that once linked up to the room she'd first fallen into, but it had been walled up, and there was no way of determining the reason. They found nothing else in the basement. By the time they got upstairs, it was dark. Jackson started a fire, and they pooled their food supplies—what he had in his bag and what she'd bought in town. They ate in silence.

"Is it all right if I sleep indoors?" she asked finally. "I'll find my own room."

"What?" He started, as if from a reverie. "Of course. Last night...I wasn't kicking you out to be a jerk. I thought you had someplace to go. If I'd known you didn't..." He shrugged and passed Tess another apple.

After a few minutes of silent eating, he said, "Downstairs, when you said I was treating you like a dumb kid, I didn't mean it like that. Sometimes I...well, I figure if I know things and others don't, then I should tell them."

"You're smart, and you like explaining things. I like learning things. It's just...the way you do it sometimes."

He nodded, flushing, as if he might have heard a similar sentiment before.

"You'd make a good teacher," she said. "Is that what you're planning to be?"

He looked startled, then shook his head. "No."

She waited in the vain hope he'd tell her what he *did* plan to become. Of course, he didn't. After another minute of silence, she decided to take another poke.

"Are you backpacking?" she asked.

"Hmm?"

She pointed to his pack. "I asked if you're backpacking."

A pause, as if reluctant to answer, then a simple "Yes."

Silence ticked by so loudly that Tess swore she could hear a clock somewhere in the bowels of the dark house. The firelight flickered through the room, casting dancing shadows over the walls.

"You're right," he said finally. "About this place. It could have been a private mental hospital that didn't operate by the rules. When you mentioned that place in Ontario, it reminded me of something I heard at one of my parents' dinners."

He shifted, getting comfortable on the old chair he'd pulled over to the fireplace. "My parents are activists. Mostly for Métis rights, but issues bleed over, and they have friends who are fighting for French rights, Native rights, provincial rights. There's a lot going on in Quebec right now.

Some people even talk about breaking away from Canada. It's an interesting time."

"Interesting in a good way?"

He rubbed his chin. "I think so. The causes are good. I'm not as involved in them as my parents are." A short laugh. "Which is the complete opposite of my classmates. They're into the social issues, and their parents think a sit-in is something you do with sick relatives. I mostly stick to my studies, but I do care about all those things—Métis, Native, French, Quebec. I help my parents out when I can. Anyway, they have dinners and people talk about social issues and politics and all that, and I remember a few months ago, they were discussing this rumor about our premier. Well, it's more than a rumor, actually, or I wouldn't be spreading it.

"In Quebec, the provincial government supports orphanages, and the federal government supports hospitals, including psychiatric ones. Apparently, the premier is relabeling orphanages as hospitals and, in some cases, shipping orphans to mental hospitals, saying they're mentally deficient."

"Wh-what?" Tess shot upright. "They can't do that."

"The government gets away with some crazy stuff, Tess. If it's true—and I have no reason to believe it isn't—then I guess I can't say something shady—or even criminal— couldn't have happened in this house."

Tess sat in stunned silence, thinking about what he'd said. "How can they do that? With the orphans?"

"I didn't mean to upset you." He went quiet. "I should have realized I would. It sounds bad, but orphanages aren't exactly the best places to live under any circumstances. Or so I've heard. Yours..." He looked at her. "You seem normal." He cleared his throat. "I mean, obviously you're normal. I mean physically all right—and well educated, if they're teaching you French. That's not common in Ontario, is it?"

"No."

"Was it all right? The Home? I'm sure it wouldn't be great, obviously. And it looks like maybe you didn't get a lot to eat."

She gave him a look. "That's just me. I'm small."

"Oh." Another throat clearing. "Not abnormally small. Just tiny. I thought maybe...well, I guess I was jumping to conclusions. I'm not exactly a big guy myself, and I eat lots, so..." He looked at her. "I'm not making this any better, am I?"

"No." A brief smile. "But it's kind of fun to watch you try." She took a bite of her apple. "The Home was fine. Orphanages are like mental hospitals, I think—people get ideas of them based on books and movies, and most aren't anything like that. It wasn't perfect, of course. Lots of rules. Sharing everything. But there wasn't anything *wrong* with it. We got a good education. Better than most kids in town. It could be disjointed though. Most of the teachers were temporary, and they had their areas of expertise and we just learned whatever they wanted to teach."

"Like Métis history."

She smiled. "Like that. I have the basics though. Solid basics, with some bonuses, like French. Did...?" She was going to ask if he'd studied English in school but switched to less personal phrasing. "Do they teach English here? Is it mandatory?"

"Education here is a mess," he said, easing into lecture mode. "Did I mention lots of changes? That's part of it. Right now, each board sets its own program, issues its own diplomas based on its own criteria—fifteen *hundred* boards. That's nuts. There's a commission doing a report, trying to change that. Part of the problem is that French isn't an official language in Canada, so if you want to go past high school, you'd better speak English. In the smaller towns, like this one, everyone speaks French. They don't learn English."

"So they should teach it."

"No," he said carefully. "I would say Quebec children *should* learn the *basics* of English, because knowing extra languages is always beneficial. Like you learning French. But the solution isn't to teach more English. It's to *accept* more French. To let us *be* French. It's like being Métis. It's more than just biology or language. It's a culture."

She nodded. "Is that why your parents made sure you learned English? Because until things change, you'll need it for university?"

"Partly. I went to a private school, and they taught it there, but I didn't really need that. My mom's from Ontario. English is her first language. French is Dad's. We speak both at home."

"And you know a third one. Cree?"

"Right," he said. "That's more like you and French. I know enough to carry on a halting conversation. Mamé, my dad's mother, speaks it, and she lives with us. She speaks French, but she'll switch to Cree to teach me."

"You and your sisters? You mentioned you have some."

"Two. They're a lot older than me. Married with kids."

She grinned. "So you're the baby?"

He made a face. "I guess. It doesn't feel like that. My parents are pretty liberal. Once we're old enough to act like adults, we're treated like adults. All the freedom and independence we want, as long as we're responsible about it. Like me being here. They're fine with it. They trust me." He glanced at his watch. "It's almost eleven. We should find you something to sleep on. I don't suppose you brought a blanket?"

She shook her head. "I wasn't planning to rough it. But I can spread out my clothes and sleep on those."

"No, there's a drawer of blankets in one of the bedrooms. We'll get you one that isn't too moth-eaten."

❧

Tess took an old blanket and settled into the large pantry. An odd place to pick as a bedroom, but Jackson insisted.

"There aren't any windows here," he said.

"Which means it'll be too dark."

"The moon will shine in through the doorway, and I'll give you the flashlight."

She looked around the pantry. "Why here?"

"Because there aren't any windows." Impatience edged into his voice, clearly frustrated by her inability to see what seemed obvious to him. After a moment of silence, he said, "No one can see you're in here alone."

"Who would see me?"

He didn't answer, as if again waiting for her to jump to the right conclusion. This time she did.

"Steve? The man who chased me? You don't think he'd find me up here—"

"Are you going to take that chance?"

He was right, and she conceded it with a nod. "I'll stay in here."

"I would give you my switchblade, but you don't know how to use one, and that makes it more dangerous. It can be taken and turned against you."

"All right."

"If you're going to be out in the world on your own, you should have a weapon though. You just need to learn how to use it first."

"All right."

He started to leave then, but stopped and turned. "We have to do something about Etienne. At the very least, inform the police."

"I don't want to."

"You'd rather let him go after another girl? Give it some thought. We'll talk in the morning."

Tess knew she should give it thought—but as soon as he left and she lay down, other thoughts consumed her. Ones of the house. Of the small rooms. Of the boxes.

She listened to Jackson in the other room as he settled into his blankets. He tossed and turned for a few minutes, but the day's work had taken its toll, and soon the swish and thump of his movements stopped and deep breathing took their place.

Tess glanced toward the basement door. The answers were down there, and now that he'd drifted off, she was free to get them in her own way.

Her own way.

She rubbed the goose bumps rising on her arms. Her own way did not mean searching for a clue they'd missed. It meant searching for the clues Jackson couldn't see. Ghosts. Visions.

Is that what she thought they were now? Ghosts and visions? Not madness?

Tess didn't know. She'd heard someone last night, speaking French, crying for help. Then they'd discovered that the house seemed to have been used for mental patients. That there were rooms like the ones in her nightmares. Boxes like the ones in her nightmares.

Nightmares? Or memories?

Or hallucinations? Signs that she belonged in a place like this. That she was crazy.

There was a way to answer that, wasn't there? Go downstairs. See what happened. If she saw something, she could investigate and get two kinds of answers from it—one that told her what had happened in this house and one that told her she wasn't crazy. Or she could investigate, find nothing and get the answer she dreaded—that she was crazy. It was still an answer, though, and she wanted that, whichever way it went.

So all she had to do was go downstairs. Into the pitch-dark basement, with no stairs, with walled-in rooms and empty closets and boxes that looked like caskets. Go down there and purposely try to call forth terrifying visions.

She shivered convulsively, pulling the blankets tighter, wrapping herself in them. The chill still seeped into her bones.

Finally, she threw off the blanket, got up and walked into the library, where Jackson slept. If he wasn't really sleeping as soundly as it seemed, that would give her the excuse she needed to stay upstairs, because if he heard her sneak into the basement, he'd be angry, and she couldn't afford to upset him. She needed his help.

Did she still *have* his help? They hadn't discussed what would happen after his day of work was over. She could offer him another five, but she realized now that the money hadn't made any difference. He had only pretended it did to fend off questions.

She wished he did need the money. That would be a clear-cut way to gain his assistance. She didn't want him to go. His French was a help, and having someone at her side meant she wasn't easy prey for men like Steve. All excellent reasons to keep him. Yet none were the real one.

Tess imagined the other girls from the orphanage here with her, watching him sleep. Some of them would giggle about how cute he was. Yes, he was cute. Still, that wasn't the reason she wanted him to stay. Seeing him asleep, all she thought about was waking him up. About going over, bending down and...kissing him? Definitely not. The very thought sent a flash of unease through her gut, confusion mingled with exhilaration and a dozen other emotions she couldn't name, most of them uncomfortable.

What Tess wanted to do was wake him up and say, *Talk to me. Just talk. I don't care what you say.*

Part of that was fear—the overwhelming feeling that she *should* go down to that basement and she was a coward if she didn't, that she'd miss the best opportunity for answers. She wanted to wake him and get him talking to chase the shadows away. Postpone the decision.

But there was more to it than mere distraction. She simply wanted to hear him talk, the sound of his voice, the look on his face, animated as he launched into whatever topic occupied his busy mind.

Talk to me. Tell me something new. About the world. About your world. About you.

That was why she wanted to wake him. Because he was a fascinating boy. Brilliant and loquacious one minute, guarded and wary the next. Rude, impatient, easily irritated. Then kind and concerned and conscientious, worried about a man who might go after girls he'd never met. A private-school boy who carried a switchblade and knew how to pick a lock, who came from a good, solid family. A loving and close family too—she could tell that by the way he talked about them.

She wanted to know more about him. And she might never get the chance. Come morning, he could be gone, and she'd never even gotten his last name.

That was life, she supposed. Real life, outside the orphanage. Outside Hope. You meet people in passing. Kind people like the old couple who'd bought her tea and the man who'd helped her buy the scarf. Or people like Steve, who she never wanted to see again but who would leave an impression forever. Or people like Jackson, who she wanted to get to know better, even though she knew that might not be her decision to make.

Tess rubbed her hands over her face and looked through the dark house toward the basement door.

This was her decision to make. Jackson would go down there in a heartbeat. Not because he was a boy, or because he was stronger or tougher, but because he wouldn't let anything stop him from getting answers.

Tess clenched the flashlight in her hand and walked to the basement door.

Seventeen

WITH THE FLASHLIGHT stuffed in her waistband,
Tess lowered herself into the basement. Then she took out
the flashlight and ventured into the basement.

She knew exactly where she wanted to go. The room with
the boxes. She found it easily enough. The basement might be
a warren of short halls and interconnected rooms, but she'd
mentally mapped it out as she'd considered coming down.
Having that map felt like having a plan. Solid and firm.

As she stepped into the room, she held her breath,
waiting for...well, she didn't know what she was waiting
for. A vision? A voice? All these years of wishing the visions
gone, and now she hoped to conjure one and had no idea if
such a thing was possible.

If it was, it didn't happen on demand. She walked into
that room and saw nothing except the four boxes. She sat
on one and waited. Long minutes ticked past. She closed
her eyes then, or tried to, but that was like closing them on

a haunted-house ride, knowing something would jump out at any moment. It didn't take long for Tess to decide to keep her eyes open.

Another twenty minutes, and not so much as a mouse skittered past. Tess rose and looked around. She opened one box, but as soon as she did, a chill slid down her spine, and she closed it fast. She walked around the room once, weaving in and out of the boxes. Then she headed into the hall.

Tess wandered through the other rooms. She'd read enough about ghosts to know people thought the best way to contact them was to open yourself up to the possibility. To radiate welcome and invitation. Which was probably much easier if your stomach wasn't tied in knots and part of you wasn't desperately hoping you *wouldn't* see anything.

After about an hour in the basement, though, Tess genuinely began wanting to see something. It was like dreading a test and then finding out it had been postponed, and feeling annoyed because she'd studied for it and she was ready *now*. With each minute that passed, she grew more frustrated, searched harder, struggled to catch a glimpse of something, *anything*.

A man walked past the end of the hall as she swung into it. Tess jerked back, jamming her fist into her mouth to keep from crying out. He disappeared through a doorway before she could get a good look.

Tess looked down the hall. The doors were closed... and they'd been open a moment ago. She and Jackson had left them all open as they'd walked through, so they'd know which rooms they'd looked inside.

Then she noticed the hallway now glowed with a sickly yellow light. She looked around. Nothing else in the hall seemed to have changed, but when she glanced down, the floor was clean. Still concrete but scrubbed, the faint lines from a mop still showing.

The man had disappeared into a room down the hall. The door was half closed, and a stronger light emanated from within. Tess tried to peek inside, but the angle wasn't quite right. She put her fingers against the door. She could feel it, cold and solid, yet when she nudged, nothing happened. She pushed harder. Still nothing.

I'm the invisible one, she thought. Like a ghost in his world. This proves it.

That wasn't exactly true. It might only prove that she *thought* she was the ghost, so in her hallucination she behaved as she expected. But she wasn't letting herself tumble down that rabbit hole. She tried the door once more and then turned sideways and wriggled through the opening, which remained as solid and unyielding as if the door was nailed in place.

Before she went through, she made some noise, testing whether the person inside could hear her. As expected, she seemed as invisible and silent as a ghost, and when she squeezed through the door with a grunt, the occupant never even turned around.

A man of about twenty-five sat at a desk, writing furiously with his back to Tess. He wore a tweed jacket, dress shirt and tie. His clothing looked a little out of date, but not unreasonably so—she'd seen old men in Hope wearing a similar cut of shirt and trousers, as if they hadn't cleared their closets in a couple of decades.

Tess looked around the room. She vaguely recalled from earlier that there'd been a desk pushed up on its side and two tables. Now the tables were gone and the desk was upright, with a proper chair, and there was a filing cabinet. On the wall hung a chalkboard displaying a hand-drawn chart of names and various codes and numbers.

Tess had no idea what the chart meant. If she had to hazard a guess, she'd say it was a list of patients and their medical data. The names were French. André W., Corrine P., Dorothée J., Jacques K., Stéphanie R.

On another wall was a calendar, turned to December 1946. The year before she was born.

She walked to the man and peered over his shoulder. He was scribbling quickly in a journal. His handwriting would be near-illegible under the best of circumstances. The fact it was in French meant she could only decipher the odd word, meaningless out of context.

Distant footsteps sounded. The man yanked open a desk drawer and slid the journal under it. When Tess crouched, she could see a leather strap stapled or nailed to the bottom of the drawer, a secret holder for the journal.

The man locked the drawer and walked to the door. He opened it and said, "Ah, Pierre." Then: "*Qu'est-ce qui ne va pas?*" What's wrong?

Another man's voice answered in French. "Stéphanie won't go in the box."

"Can you blame her?" the young man muttered, but under his breath so only Tess heard. Louder, he said, "Perhaps she needs a day off. She's making excellent progress—"

"Which is why we cannot give her a day off. I'll need your help restraining her."

The man in the office shifted his weight. "I did not agree to any use of force with the patients. I was quite clear—"

"Take it up with the doctor. I'm telling you our orders. Get Stéphanie in the box, one way or another."

The room went dark. Tess jumped, her back going to the wall. She fumbled to turn on the flashlight. When she did, she saw the room as it had been when she'd investigated with Jackson.

She walked over to the desk, on its side again, and pulled on the top drawer. It was locked.

"*Aidez-moi...*"

The voice seemed to whisper all around her, and every hair on Tess's body rose. She strained to listen.

"*Je suis désolée.*"

The voice snaked through the open door. Tess squelched the twitch of relief, the one that said, "Good, she's out *there*."

Wasn't this what she'd come downstairs for? In hopes of hearing something, seeing something?

"*Aidez-moi, s'il vous plaît.*"

Tess gripped the flashlight and walked to the door. It opened easily now, meaning she was definitely back in her own world.

"*Aidez-moi, s'il vous plaît. Je suis désolée.*"

The voice started close and then drifted, drawing her down the hall. Tess followed. The crying began, a soft sniffling. When Tess saw where it led, she rubbed the goose bumps on her arms and forced her feet to keep moving.

Tess shone the flashlight into the room. Across the boxes that looked like caskets, no matter what Jackson said. The crying stopped. Tess exhaled and adjusted her sweaty fingers on the flashlight. She glanced back toward the room with the desk and hidden journal. The drawer lock couldn't be that hard to break. Or perhaps if she removed the drawer below it…

A noise. She froze. It came again. A slow scratching. Tess swiveled, her gaze tracking the sound to one of the boxes.

No. No, no, no.

She took a slow step backward. She'd seen enough. There could be a journal in the other room. If she got that, she'd have answers. She didn't need to do this.

If she got that. If the journal was still there now, in the present time. There was a very good chance it was not.

The scratching stopped, and choked sobs began.

"*S'il vous plaît. S'il vous plaît. S'il vous plaît.*" Please, please, please.

Tess took a slow step into the room. The scratching resumed, harsh now, frantic. Coming from one of the boxes, mingled with cries and sobs, and it didn't matter that Tess thought she was hearing a ghost, an echo of the past—she heard the frantic scratching turn to pounding, saw one of the boxes shaking, and she threw herself forward. She raced to the moving box, grabbed the lid and wrenched it off, staggering with the effort, the top coming free in her hands and knocking her to the floor. She sat there, stunned, holding the huge, heavy wooden lid. Then she shoved it aside, letting it clatter to the concrete floor as she leaped to her feet and looked into the box.

It was empty.

Tess stood there, heaving breath, as she stared into the dark box. Then she lifted the flashlight and shone it inside. Empty. Completely empty.

Of course it was. She'd known there wasn't anyone actually trapped inside. Perhaps, though, she'd expected to open it and see the ghost of whoever had been crying and scratching and pounding. But the box lay empty, and the room had gone silent.

Tess turned away. As she did, her flashlight beam flitted across the discarded wooden lid. She briefly saw markings on the underside, like writing. She shone the light at it. Not writing. Brown marks and gouges, like someone had carved initials into the wood.

Carved initials? No. That wasn't what she was seeing. Not at all.

Tess dropped to her knees beside the lid and touched the gouges. They were exactly the width of her fingernails. Deep, splintered gouges, the edges dulled by time. When she moved the flashlight closer, the brown splotches turned reddish. Dried blood. That's what she was seeing. Bloodied scratches in the wood.

Eighteen

THE ROOM WENT dark as Tess envisioned herself trapped in that box herself, crying out, in French now, like the woman. *"Aidez-moi! Je suis désolée!"* Clawing at the lid, feeling hot blood drip onto her face, feeling the splintering wood digging in, the sharp pain, her nails cracking and breaking, fingers raw and bloody—

The nightmare snapped away in the blink of an eye. Tess ran her fingers over the gouges as her heart thudded so hard she could barely draw breath.

"Not me," she whispered. "It wasn't me. But who?"

"Stéphanie won't go in the box."

"Can you blame her?"

"Aidez-moi, s'il vous plaît. Je suis désolée." Once again the voice floated in from the hall, knocking Tess from her memories.

She rose and turned toward the door. This time she didn't hesitate. She started for the hall, resolve slowing her heart rate.

She'd seen the worst—her nightmare come to life—and she'd survived. Whatever happened now, she could handle it.

Tess strode down the hall, flashlight beam ping-ponging off the walls. She followed the crying to…

The room with the closet that was not a closet at all. The one where she'd been momentarily trapped. The crying came from that closet across the room. Then, as she listened, a long, slow scrape, a single nail against wood.

"*Laissez-moi sortir.*" Let me out.

"*S'il vous plaît, laissez-moi sortir.*" Please let me out.

Fists pounded the door, making Tess jump and drop the flashlight. It hit the concrete and went out. She scrambled for it as the pounding continued, seeming to rock the entire room. Her shaking hands found the flashlight. She flicked the switch, but it was already in the *On* position. She turned it off and on, whispering, "No, please, no." She banged it against her leg, and it blinked once, then came back on.

The pounding stopped. Tess crouched there, flashlight aimed at the door. Then, again, one fingernail slowly scraped down it. A voice whispered, almost too faint to hear.

"*Laissez-moi sortir.*" Let me out.

"*Je serai obéissante.*" I will behave.

A chill slid down Tess's back at those last words.

Another slow scratch on the wood, and Tess squeezed her eyes shut, wishing for the pounding again. This was so much more chilling. After a moment, she inhaled deeply and pushed up. She walked to the door.

"Can you hear me?" she asked. Then, in French, "*Vous m'entendez?*"

Quiet crying followed.

"*Je veux vous aider.*" I want to help you. "*Parlez-moi, et je vous aiderai.*" Speak to me, and I will help you.

No answer. She didn't expect one, but she'd wanted to make the effort. If this was a ghost, and if she could hear Tess, surely she would reply to that. If she did not, it proved these "visions" could not communicate.

Tess turned the handle and pulled open the door. Inside she saw nothing but darkness, and the crying had stopped. As with the box, as soon as the door opened the ghost—or whatever it was—disappeared.

Tess stepped inside. This time she was careful to keep the door propped open with her foot. She shone the flashlight over the inside of the door. Sure enough, there were scratches. That's what this room was, this tiny room with no shelves and no rod: an upright casket-sized box.

She fingered the scratches. No blood here, but—

A shriek sounded right outside the room. Tess startled and lost her footing. The door swung shut. She pushed.

It wouldn't open.

Tess swung the light down. There wasn't a handle on the inside. Of course there wasn't. She shoved the door harder, struggling to control her pounding heart.

It couldn't be locked. There *was* no lock. It was just stuck. All she had to do was—

The flashlight went out.

Tess banged it against her leg. She flicked it on and off. Her pulse raced, her breath coming fast and shallow, but she kept telling herself she would not panic. *Would not panic.* When the light didn't turn on, she kicked at the door. Then she threw her shoulder against it.

Another shriek, this one right at her ear. Tess screamed. She couldn't help it. She heard her screams echoing the ghost's, and she doubled over, eyes squeezed shut.

The woman kept screaming. Horrible screams of terror. Absolute terror. Like nothing Tess had ever heard before. Then the room tilted. Tilted backward, and she knew what was happening and told herself it *couldn't* be happening. That it was impossible. But all the reasoning in the world didn't change what she felt. Or what she heard. The room tipping backward. The screams of the terrified woman, mingling with her own. Then somehow, over that, the patter of dirt on the wooden lid.

Tess screamed until her throat was raw. She pounded on the lid. Pounded and pounded, until her fists ached, and then she began to gasp for air. Gasping, wheezing, fighting to breathe, until—

A whoosh of air. Light. Flickering light overhead. She looked up to see a flame. Behind the flame, a hand. Then a face, shadow and firelight playing over it.

"Tess!"

A hand grabbed hers, and she felt a moment of complete disorientation. One second she'd been lying on her back, and now she was looking up at a light and a stranger's face, and she wasn't lying down at all but huddled on the floor.

"Tess." Then "Thérèse," the voice urgent as she was pulled out into a room. A curse and a quickly waved hand, the flame going out. The hand released her, and the voice told her to hold on, just hold on. The scratch and hiss of a struck match. The face returned, and with it her shock fell away, and she saw Jackson with a match in one hand, her arm in the other, his face lowered to hers, saying, "What happened? Tess? Can you hear me?"

She shook him off and backed away.

"Whoa! No. Hold on." He grabbed for her again, but she backed against the wall and stared at him.

What is he thinking? What must *he be thinking?* Shame filled her.

"I think you were sleepwalking," he said. "Do you do that?"

Yes, she wanted to say. *I sleepwalk and I came down here, and I don't know what happened, but I got myself in that closet and I must have been having some kind of nightmare. I'm sorry I disturbed you. Thank you for coming.*

Such an easy lie. But when she opened her mouth, she heard herself saying instead, "Ghosts. I see ghosts. I saw them, down here, and—"

She clapped her hand over her mouth. He stared at her, his face screwed up, and in that expression she saw not confusion but revulsion. She darted past him.

"Whoa! No! Tess!"

She kept running, tearing down the pitch-black hall, her hands bumping and scraping against the walls as she felt her way. Jackson ran behind her, yelling for her to hold up, that she was going to trip, going to hurt herself.

She reached the rope and started up. He was far enough back for her to make it almost to the top before he reached her.

"Tess! Hold on! You can't—"

A sudden blast of light illuminated the way. Jackson muttered, "Finally," and shone the flashlight beam up at her. "Whatever happened—"

The flashlight went out again. She was at the top of the rope now, the moonlight coming through the windows enough for her to see by. She raced to the back door and opened it. Then she stopped. She turned. Jackson tore into the library after her. Seeing her there, in the doorway, he skidded to a halt.

"Thérèse," he panted. "Just—"

"I'm all right."

"No, obviously you are not—"

"No, I am. I'm all right. I went down to explore, and I got stuck in that room. The flashlight broke and I panicked. I'm—I'm going to leave. You don't need to come after me. I'm fine."

"The hell you are." His face gathered in a scowl. "You're racing out in the middle of the night. That's not fine, and I *will* come after—"

"No. Please." Her voice shook, and she struggled to keep it even, frantic to convince him she was all right, to let her leave. Let her take her humiliation and panic and just go.

He stepped toward her. She backed away.

"Tess," he said, his voice low, "I don't want to chase you."

"Then don't."

"Talk to me."

She shook her head vehemently, hair lashing her face.

"Then I'm going to follow you," he said. "To make sure you're safe. Either I follow or we talk."

Talk. She remembered standing in the same doorway where he was now, watching him sleep, wishing he'd stir so she could talk to him.

She imagined a perfect scenario, where she'd blurt out what had happened downstairs and he'd tilt his head in that thoughtful way, the gears of his mind turning, and say, "That's interesting. Well, it could be..." Then he'd list all the possibilities, as if she had described symptoms of a physical ailment.

She imagined that and her knees shuddered, weak with the relief. That's what she wanted. To blurt it out and analyze the facts, and not *be* analyzed herself, not be treated as a freak, treated as crazy.

Then she thought of his face in the basement. Revulsion. She was certain that's what she'd seen. She imagined the scenario again, where she'd blurt out what had happened in the basement and this time he'd back away, disgusted and a little bit afraid. When she ran, he would not follow. He'd want the crazy girl as far away as possible.

"I—I'm going to leave," she said.

"Then I'm going to follow."

"I don't want—"

"If you really wanted to run, you'd be gone by now."

That stung, and she straightened. "I stopped because I'm trying to be mature about this. I don't want to race off and make you chase me. I'm asking you not to."

"Something happened down there, and you're upset, and if I wasn't going to let you sleep outside alone tonight, I'm sure as hell not going to let you tear through the forest at 2:00 AM. That man—"

"—is not lurking in the forest waiting for me," she said with a hint of exasperation, some of the fear sliding away.

"Are you sure? I'm not. So I won't take the chance. You go, I follow. Or we talk."

"I don't want to."

"You said ghosts. That you saw…" He trailed off. "No, you said you *see* ghosts *and* that you saw them. Which means you spotted one downstairs, and you've seen them in the past. Is that right?"

He said it matter-of-factly, but she still tensed, not wanting to slide into the trap of thinking he might actually listen to her.

She could back out now. Avoid all potential embarrassment by claiming she'd been sleepwalking and had had a nightmare about ghosts. He would accept it, and they could continue on as if nothing had happened.

The easy way out. The dishonest, cowardly way out.

"I don't know if I see ghosts," she said carefully. She steeled herself and met his gaze. "I'm not crazy."

"Did I say you were?"

"You will when I explain."

His face hardened. "Which you know for a fact? You met me a day ago, Thérèse. Might I suggest you don't know me nearly well enough to jump to any conclusion about how I'll react."

"You're right. I'm sorry."

His face stayed tight for a moment, and then he nodded. "I would never call you crazy. Well, I might, but not in that way. Not seriously. That word gets tossed around, and I'm guilty of using it too, but it isn't the same thing and you know that."

"What if I *am* crazy?" she asked quietly.

"It could be schizophrenia," he said. "Which does strike in early adulthood and can manifest in visual and auditory—" He cut himself short and flushed. "Sorry. You don't need that."

"No," she said. "Go on. Please."

When he hesitated, she said, "I want to know."

"I'm not saying that's the automatic diagnosis for anyone who sees visions. But I'll be honest: if that's what it sounded like, I would suggest you get help. It's a serious illness, and it can be controlled. However..." He studied her for at least thirty seconds before saying, "I just accused you of not knowing me very well after a twenty-four-hour acquaintance, so I'm not going to jump in and say, 'You're obviously not schizophrenic,' but I haven't seen any other signs of it. You aren't paranoid or delusional—I had to convince you that jerk really was after you. Your thinking is clear enough. Same as your speech, even if you could use more French lessons."

A small smile, as if he was trying to calm her. When she didn't reply, he continued, "You aren't violent, and your hygiene is just fine—you harped on me enough about showering to prove that."

She still said nothing. Her mind spun, finding something to grasp but afraid to do it, afraid to trust it.

His mother was a psychologist. He seemed to know a lot about mental illness. He'd made it clear earlier that he didn't treat the afflicted like crazy people who should be locked away and forgotten. If she wanted someone to talk to—and to get an honest and unbiased reaction—Jackson could give it.

Still, she held back. She wanted the truth. What she didn't want, if she was being perfectly honest, was Jackson thinking there was something wrong with her. She'd spent her life being Tess Stacy, orphan girl. That label had colored how everyone in Hope treated her, how everyone she'd ever met treated her. The only worse label would be Tess Stacy, crazy girl.

For once in her life, she had the chance to be simply a girl. A girl with a boy, and it didn't matter if she exasperated him and frustrated him and annoyed him. It didn't matter if they would never be more than a boy and a girl passing at this point in their lives. Whatever he thought of her, it was based on *her*—how she acted. No labels. Just Tess Stacy.

"Tess?" He took a slow step toward her. When she tensed, he stopped and lowered his voice another notch, his accent adding a soothing lilt to his voice, like he was coaxing a stray cat from the doorway. "You said you're not crazy, and I agree. But it sounds as if you're not sure *what* this is and whether it's a problem. You need answers."

It was as if he'd pulled the thought from her mind, and she nodded. "I do."

"Then come inside and talk to me."

She gripped the doorjamb and looked over her shoulder into the woods. No answers there. Just more darkness. She'd had enough of that for one night.

She followed him into the house.

Nineteen

THEY RETURNED TO the library. Tess huddled on the chair, her shoes off, feet pulled up under her, as Jackson started the fire. He took a couple of apples from his bag.

"We're getting to the bottom," he said, holding one of them up. "They're a little battered. Is that all right?"

She nodded, and he tossed it over.

"I'll need to go into town tomorrow," he said. "To buy food and a new flashlight."

"I'm sorry about the flashlight. I dropped it."

"That wasn't an accusation, Tess. It might just be the batteries anyway."

She nodded. She hadn't noticed his tone—she'd been paying too much attention to his words. *He'd* go into town. Not *they*. This partnership would end come morning.

Her only consolation was that she doubted her behavior tonight had scared him off. He'd never had any intention of sticking with her past morning.

"Whenever you're ready," he said. Now his tone was nonchalant, trying not to rush her, but he couldn't disguise the note of his usual impatience.

"I've always seen them," she said. "For as long as I can remember."

"Ghosts?" He answered his own question before she could. "No, you said you aren't sure they're ghosts. But you see people? Visions?"

"There are two kinds," she said. "Some seem like ghosts. I see people from another time. But I can't communicate with them in any way. They don't notice me. They're just... doing whatever they're doing. Completely unaware of me, even if I talk to them or stand in their path."

He nodded and said nothing.

"The other kind is like *I'm* the ghost. One second I'm here, in the regular world. The next, I'm in a different time, with people from it."

"Can you communicate with those people?"

She shook her head. "It's the same. Except in those ones, I can't move anything, like opening a door."

"Is it the same place? I mean, if you were to pop into one of those visions now, would you be *here*? In this library?"

She nodded. "Exactly where I am now. Only the time period changes."

"Always into the past?"

"Yes. It happened downstairs. Tonight. I...I went down to see if anything would happen. I've never done that. But I thought maybe I could get answers if I did. If I envision one

thing, and we find a completely different answer, then..."
She squirmed in the chair. "Then I know for sure it's not real. That I'm hallucinating."

"You said the people don't talk to you. Don't ask you to do anything."

She paused. "I heard a woman downstairs. When I fell through yesterday, and again tonight. She was asking for help, but when I answered, she just kept asking."

"She's not asking *you* then. You're just hearing her cries for help because that's what she's doing. Like the others. They just keep doing what they're doing. Paying no attention to you."

"Yes."

"If you were schizophrenic, they'd be asking you to do something. Demanding things or talking to you."

"Wouldn't ghosts do the same? Why show themselves if they aren't going to communicate?"

He said nothing.

"Do you believe in ghosts?" she asked.

He considered for a minute. "Logically, no. I've heard too many stories about grieving relatives hoping for contact. Or groaning pipes and bad electrical connections. I don't completely deny the possibility though. And I've certainly heard stories where ghosts don't interact. They're just there. It's the 'stepping into another time' part that doesn't fit. You said you heard voices last night. Did you see anyone?"

"No, I just heard a woman crying. Asking for help. Saying she was sorry. Tonight...tonight I followed the voice. It led to the room with the boxes. She was..."

Tess started shivering convulsively.

Jackson leaped to his feet. "Tess?"

"She was in one of the boxes. Trapped. I opened it. I knew she wasn't really there, but I had to open it. The box was empty."

"And the crying stopped?"

She nodded. "For a few minutes. Then it started again, from outside the room. I followed it into one of the rooms with a closet. I stepped in to look around. I was propping the door open with my foot, but I heard a scream and it startled me. The door shut, and I couldn't get it open. I know there's no lock. It just—it wouldn't open."

Jackson stiffened. His hand dropped to his pocket, pulling out the switchblade. "Like someone was holding it closed."

"I don't think so. I'd slipped into another time, so I couldn't move the door. But there was no way to know it was a different time, meaning I didn't realize what was going on. So I panicked. I was trapped. That's what those little rooms were for. Locking people in. Like the boxes."

He frowned over at her.

"They were restraints," she said. "Like straitjackets."

He shook his head. "Psychiatric hospitals *did* use things like that—cribs—but they were outlawed more than fifty years ago, and they weren't like those boxes. They were... well, cribs. With slats so the person inside could see out. Even that's horrible. Those boxes?" He shook his head. "They'd never use something like that."

"They did," she said. "There are gouges on the inside. Bloody gouges from the woman trying to claw her way out.

That's what I heard. She was scratching in the box and pleading to be let out. When I opened it, I saw the marks. There and inside the closet."

He stared at her.

"You can see for yourself," she said.

"Then they're real."

"That's what I said. There are gouges—"

"No, your visions. If you heard someone inside the box, crying and scratching to get out, and then you opened it and saw scratch marks, that means you aren't imagining these things. They really are happening. Well, no, they *did* happen. It's like the opposite of a psychic ability. Instead of seeing the future, you see the past."

He went quiet, as if lost in his thoughts. Tess didn't interrupt. She was busy thinking too. This hadn't occurred to her. If she'd heard a thing and then proved it happened, that was the answer she'd been searching for, wasn't it? Proof that she wasn't hallucinating? That somehow she'd opened a door into the past and peeked or stepped through. Unless...

"Can you check the box and the closet?" she asked.

"Hmm?"

"Check to make sure you see what I did. So we'll know."

"Good idea," he said and pushed to his feet.

✎

The scratches were there. Old ones, caked with dried blood, exactly as she'd seen them. No blood in the closet, just the scratches. And dents too—she saw those now. Dents as if someone had pounded on the door.

Jackson found signs of locks on the outside of both the box and the closet. They'd been removed, but the holes were there.

"I...don't get it," Jackson said, fingering the holes. "Why would someone do this?"

"Restraint."

He shook his head. "Restraint presumes the woman was trying to hurt herself. That's common in psychiatric care, like I said. You don't want a patient harming herself or others. Restraints are a last resort, but if they're needed, they are used. Sedatives. Straitjackets. Padded rooms. But the people in these *hurt* themselves trying to get out. They panicked. It makes no sense to restrain someone in a box where they can move but can't see anything. Panic is guaranteed. It would trigger the fear of being buried alive."

"What?"

He didn't seem to notice the sharpness in her voice and replied calmly, still examining the door. "Fear of being buried alive. Poe practically made his career writing about it. It's a common phobia."

"It is?"

"Sure. That's the basis of claustrophobia. Even when you know rationally that you can get out, there's a primitive part of your brain that doesn't care." He glanced over at her, lit by candlelight. "Have you ever been falling asleep and your whole body flails?"

She nodded.

"It's called a hypnagogic jerk. People think it dates back to primates and a fear of falling—out of trees or whatever. When you're about to fall asleep and your body goes limp, sometimes that primitive part of the brain misinterprets it as falling."

"Is there anything you don't know?"

She meant it as a compliment, but he tensed, averting his gaze, his jaw tightening.

"I don't mean—" she began.

"It's all right," he said gruffly. "I go off sometimes. I know. I'll watch it."

"No. I like it." She felt her cheeks flush and was happy for the flickering candlelight. "I mean, I like learning. Especially interesting stuff like that."

He nodded and busied himself checking the inside of the door, clearly uncomfortable with the turn the conversation had taken, and she cursed herself. It didn't matter if she liked hearing him lecture—pointing out that he *did* lecture drew attention to something that others must *not* have appreciated.

"Back to the subject," she said.

"Yes." The word came on an audible hiss of relief. "I was saying that restraining someone this way wouldn't be therapeutic. It's torture. Which makes me wonder if this place"—he looked around—"isn't what we thought it was. Not a hospital but…" He rubbed the back of his neck, uncomfortable again but in a different way. "You said you hear women.

There are people, like that jerk we ran into, who kidnap them for…bad things."

"This isn't that."

"We don't know—"

"It's something to do with medical treatment." She told him about the man she'd seen and the calendar and the conversation she'd overheard.

"That doesn't necessarily mean it was a hospital," he said. "But it doesn't sound like…the other thing." He glanced over. "You said he was writing in a journal?"

"I did. And I know where he put it."

Twenty

ON THE WAY to the basement office, Tess began to backtrack from what she'd said. Of course, there was no way of knowing that the journal would be there. In fact, it probably wasn't. If the man had hidden it, he'd have taken it when he left.

"If it's not there then it's not there, Tess," Jackson said as he walked ahead, carrying the candle. "It doesn't mean I'll doubt the rest of what you said. You already proved it with the scratches."

He picked the lock on the drawer and checked underneath it while Tess held the candle. The strap was there, but it was impossible to see if it still held a book, and Tess barely breathed as he reached in and pulled out...the journal.

Jackson turned to the first page, squinting and scowling. "His handwriting's awful."

"Reading it by candlelight doesn't help. Let's get upstairs near the fire."

Once back in the library, Jackson settled on the hearth. Tess tried not to read over his shoulder. Then she tried not to pace. She had equally little success with both, and after about five minutes, he scowled at her. "Sit. You're blocking my light."

Which was impossible, considering she wasn't between him and the fire. Still, she sat. And fidgeted, until she couldn't stand it any longer.

"What does it say?"

"Medical stuff."

"I figured that. What kind?"

"Psychiatry."

Tess let out a sigh. "You're not telling me anything I didn't already know."

"Then stop asking."

She bent over his shoulder, getting in his light for real now.

"Thérèse..."

"If you aren't going to tell me..." She reached for the book.

He snatched the journal away. "Can we not fight over a paper product in front of a blazing fire?"

She resisted the urge to fold her arms and say, *It's mine. I found it first.* Immature but true. She settled on: "I'm the one who needs answers here, Jackson. It's fine that you're curious, but what happened here is kind of important to me."

He closed the journal and looked up at her. "About that. Did we have a talk earlier about honesty?"

She turned his scowl back on him. "I'm not five."

"I never said—"

"Don't talk to me like I am then. I can't be more than a year younger than you, and I might not be quite as smart, but I'd appreciate it if you didn't treat me like an idiot."

A sigh. "I'm not—"

"You are." She mimicked his words. *"Did we have a talk earlier about honesty?"*

"All right. Maybe I shouldn't have worded it like that. But the fact remains that you have to be honest with me. If I'm helping you get answers, I need to know the whole picture. You should have told me what you heard last night. You should have told me you were going downstairs tonight and why."

"No."

His brows rose. "What?"

"No, I shouldn't have. Last night you hauled me up and kicked me out. Imagine what you'd have said if I told you I heard voices down there. Maybe I shouldn't have gone into the basement alone tonight, but do you know how many people I've told about these things before you? One. I've been seeing these visions all my life, and I have told exactly one person."

"You mean recently. Since you grew up."

"No, I mean since forever."

He shook his head. "As a child, you would have told someone. That's natural. They would have dismissed it as imaginary friends, so you've forgotten that you mentioned it. But when you were little, you wouldn't have known that you shouldn't talk about it."

"I did."

"Tess…"

"All my life, I've been terrified of anyone finding out. My gut has always told me to keep it a secret, so I have, and the only other person I've ever told is my best friend, and only because he—"

"He?"

"Yes, *he*," she snapped. "Because I knew he wouldn't judge me. I can't say the same for you, and the only reason I explained was because you caught me, and I decided I wouldn't lose anything by telling you. So in hindsight, yes, I should have told you about that Steve guy before you interviewed him. But this? No. It was not pertinent to the investigation, and I did not put you in any danger by failing to tell you."

"You put yourself in danger."

"That was my choice. Now, what does that journal say?"

He looked as if he wanted to argue the matter further but seemed unable to find a basis.

"Just read it to me," she said.

"Fine." He lifted the book into the firelight. "*October 5. Today J. showed signs of improvement. We decreased his dosage and implemented a strict dietary regimen of raw vegetables, fruits and lean meats. While I have my doubts this will help his mental condition, it may improve his overall health and strengthen his mind to fight his depression. This afternoon, P. taught me to play euchre, and we are hoping to encourage*

Dr. T. to join us. Later, I sat outside with a novel. I find the country air most refreshing and—" Jackson looked over at her. "Shall I continue? Or may I skim and find information that's actually useful?"

"It's all like that?"

"Mostly. It isn't a record of deep, dark secrets, Tess. It's an actual journal, apparently by a young doctor who was involved in a project here."

"Project?"

"Don't ask me what kind. Obviously, treating mental illness, primarily depression it seems, but that's all—"

"That's something," she said. "More than we had. Go ahead and skim, but when you get anything to add to the picture, tell me."

"*Oui*, mademoiselle."

After about an hour, Tess made him put the book down. Reading cramped, faded handwriting by firelight was a struggle, and by then he was blinking hard and wincing as if suffering from a headache, though he wouldn't admit it.

"So the writer is a young doctor of psychiatry," she said. "He was here doing what seems to be legitimate research on willing patients."

"Right, though I can't imagine..." He shook his head. "We don't know exactly what they were doing, and when I tried skipping ahead, it didn't make any sense. We'll stick to the facts. They were doing psychiatric experiments with primarily—but not exclusively—depressive patients. So far, everything seems to be going fine. He's happy with their progress. He's satisfied with their methods...which he doesn't explain."

His not explaining was the most frustrating part. As Jackson pointed out, all research was confidential— you didn't want a rival stealing it. Even if you were testing a method of treatment, which you'd share later with other professionals, the fact that you'd discovered it was huge. You could publish lots of articles on it.

"Those articles pay well?" Tess asked.

Jackson laughed softly. "No, they don't pay at all."

"So they compete to write articles they don't make money on?"

"Publish or perish." He caught her look and laughed again. "*Career* death. It's complicated. I know lots of academics, through my parents. You do research. You get it published. You get grants and do the lecture circuits, and that pays, but it certainly doesn't make you rich. It's all about the pursuit of knowledge. If you want to do that for a living, you need to get published."

"Is that what you want to do?"

"Hmm?"

"Become an academic? A professor?"

Earlier, when she'd asked if he wanted to be a teacher, he'd looked startled, as if he'd never considered it. Now when she asked this, an odd look passed over his face, almost wistful, before he shook it off with a gruff "No, nothing like that," then went on. "We know it's psychiatric research, and it's connected to McGill, because he mentions going down to the university to talk to someone in the psychology department." He drummed his fingers on the book cover. "We should go to McGill."

"The university?" She wanted to say, *Is that the right move?* Rush back to Montreal based on a line in a journal? But then she realized he'd said *they* should go there. Together, meaning he was intrigued enough by this mystery that he wasn't abandoning her at daybreak.

"We could do that," she said slowly.

"McGill is a research school," he said. "I know people in the psych department. There's also someone in parapsychology I'd like to talk to."

"Parapsychology?"

"It's the study of paranormal phenomena. Clairvoyance, reincarnation, telepathy…"

"There's a field for that?"

"It's not an official one. Not at McGill. I just know a prof who does research in it, mostly exploring people's reactions to it. But he knows all the various psychic abilities, so I thought…"

He was talking about her visions. About getting answers.

Jackson cleared his throat. "Obviously, that's not a priority. It would just be something to check on while we're there. My suggestion would be to take another look around the house in daylight. Then we can walk to town for breakfast.

I'll read more of the journal on the way, and if I find anything to suggest there are more answers here than at McGill, we'll come back after we restock our supplies. Otherwise, we head for the city. Does that work?"

It did.

Twenty-One

ANOTHER RUN THROUGH the house proved
pointless. They'd surveyed the books, separately. They'd
searched the main level, separately and together. They'd thor-
oughly scouted the basement the day before. If the house held
more secrets, they were hidden like the journal had been, and
to examine every nook and cranny would take days.

By eight the next morning they were heading for town.
When Jackson said he would read the journal on the way, he
meant that literally. He read as he walked. Tess had tried that
before, with a novel too engrossing to leave, but she'd tripped
and bumped into things often enough to decide that reading
was best left as a sedentary occupation. Jackson seemed an
expert, noticing obstacles before she could say a word.

Jackson didn't stop reading even when they reached the
village. Gaze still on the journal, he handed her a dollar bill,
grunted, "Get me whatever" and settled onto the curb.

Tess managed to obtain breakfast without incident. She wanted to believe that a day with Jackson had vastly improved her French, but the shop clerks here were simply more patient with her than the girl in Montreal had been. The *boulanger* had even used the opportunity to practice his rudimentary English and given her a bag of day-olds free of charge. It was, she had to admit, a different experience than Jackson's.

She stopped in two more shops, filling her bag with food for the day. In the first, she'd asked to use the washroom—after making purchases—so she could clean up. She'd left her boots packed because they weren't conducive to long walks, but she had tied the scarf in her hair again, and by the time she returned to Jackson, she felt more like herself. He didn't even look up from the journal, just stayed on the curb and distractedly took whatever food she handed him, eating the bread and jam without a word. Only when he'd finished the bread did he snap the book shut.

"McGill is our best bet," he said. "The writer continues to be cagey about the experiments, but all the doctors involved in the project graduated from McGill's medical school. He refers to the man in charge of the experiment as Dr. K. If I had to hazard a guess, I'd say Dr. K. was a professor at McGill, and they came together under him. That's usually how it works."

"We'll go to McGill then."

The only way to get to the bus stop was the same way Tess had arrived—hitch a ride. It was safer with Jackson and in broad daylight. The road was busier too. But it took a long time to get a car to stop, and with each one that sped past, Jackson's mood dropped. Finally, though, a van full of hippies pulled over. They were going all the way to the town with bus service. Their license plate was from Ontario, and they spoke English.

"Only got one seat," the girl in the front passenger seat said, then added with a giggle, "but I'm sure you kids won't mind getting cozy."

"I'll sit on the floor," Jackson mumbled to Tess.

The van door swung open to let out a fog of what didn't smell like cigarette smoke. Tess turned to Jackson and whispered, "Is that marijuana?" He didn't answer, just kept his face rigid and gave her a nudge that bordered on a shove. Tess climbed in, trying not to cough from the smoke. There were three more people in the backseat, and a single seat at the very rear. The remaining space was crammed with tents and sleeping bags and other gear, but Jackson cleared enough space to hunker down.

"Not going to sit on your boyfriend's lap?" one of the men in the backseat said.

"He isn't my boyfriend."

"Well, he might be, if you sit on his lap."

The men laughed. The woman up front reached back and smacked the man who'd spoken, telling him to hush, then looked at Tess. "You don't listen to them. You're just kids. Friendship is fine. Even if he is cute." She winked at Jackson, who only stared at a backpack, as if he couldn't hear her. His jaw was set in that way Tess had come to know meant *Don't bother me*. But as the van lurched forward, the smoke swirling around them, she couldn't help leaning down and whispering, "Is it safe? To drive with…that?"

"No." He caught her look of horror and his stony expression cracked, as if he'd realized he probably shouldn't be so blunt. "We'll be fine. Just keep your seat belt on."

"You don't have one."

He waved off her concern, that mask falling into place again as he withdrew. He stared at the backpack with an unblinking gaze, every muscle stiff, as if braced for the inevitable crash.

Why did we get in if it was dangerous? she wanted to ask, but as soon as she thought that, she knew the answer. Because no one else had stopped.

She didn't say anything, but she must have given off some kind of vibe, because after a minute he snapped out of it and said gruffly, "We'll be fine. They've come this far." Which meant, presuming the hippies had been driving like this since Ontario, it wasn't as if she and Jackson had stepped into a deathmobile. She had noticed that the "cigarette" being passed around didn't go to the driver, which was a relief.

"You want?" one of the men in the back said, holding out the joint to Tess.

"She doesn't," Jackson said curtly.

The woman in the front turned. "I think you should let your friend speak for herself. But I would agree." She took the joint. "She's too young."

When she turned back, Jackson muttered to Tess, "Sorry."

"I wouldn't have taken it," she whispered.

"I know. Just...sorry." He shifted his position, and it seemed difficult, as if he was holding himself so tight that it hurt to move.

"So, what are you?" asked the man who'd offered Tess the joint, looking at Jackson.

"A student."

The man rolled his eyes. "Don't get your back up, kid. I'm not being a jerk. I'm *interested*."

"Métis," Jackson said grudgingly. "French and Cree."

"Ooh, that's cool." The woman turned now. "Isn't Cree the one where they throw the dead in mass graves and let scavengers eat them?"

Tess swore Jackson cringed, but he just said, "No."

"Is your tribe near here?" another asked.

"I don't have a *tribe*. I'm Métis. It's a separate—"

"Do you live on a reservation? We were saying just the other day that we'd like to visit one, maybe check out the powwows."

"Yeah," the woman said. "That'd be cool. At one with nature. That's what we want. Respecting Mother Earth and—"

"I don't live on a reservation. I'm Métis. I live in the city. In the suburbs, actually, in a regular house, with my regular parents, who have regular jobs. I've never even been to a powwow."

"Bummer." The man who'd tried to pass the joint leaned forward. "But you could hook us up, couldn't you? With a tribe? We'd like to try those peyote shaman ceremonies—"

"Peyote is a cactus," Jackson said. "From Mexico. We aren't in Mexico. The Cree aren't from Mexico. I can't *hook you up* with anything or anyone. If you want to learn the culture, start with books."

"Nah," the man said. "That's for squares. We're all about *experiencing*. Life and cultures and diversity and..." He waved the joint and grinned. "Experiencing, you know?" He swiveled in his seat and held the joint out to Tess, leaning over so far he planted a hand on her knee. "You sure you don't want to try some, honey?"

Jackson plucked the man's hand from her leg. "She's sixteen. How old are you? Thirty?"

"Twenty-four, spaz. And sixteen is plenty old enough—"

"The boy's right, Ross," the woman said. "Even if he is a little touchy." She looked at Jackson. "We're not making fun of you. We're just trying to learn more about your culture."

Jackson seemed to struggle for a reply before saying evenly, "All right. If you really are interested, there's the McCord Museum in Montreal. It will give you information on Native and Métis cultures, and you can take it from there."

"You shouldn't get so defensive," the woman said. "People are just interested."

Now he seemed to struggle against a reply, settling for a brisk, wordless nod.

"Where are you all from?" Tess asked. "If it's all right to ask?"

It was, and the woman answered, diverting attention from Jackson. He eased back, not relaxing but withdrawing into his thoughts for the rest of the short ride.

Twenty-Two

"**YOU THINK** I was rude," Jackson said as they sat on the bench, waiting for the bus.

"Hmm?" Tess had been lost in thoughts of her own—namely, that she needed to call Billy for a check-in and buy postcards in Montreal.

"With those hippies. You think the woman was right. That I was getting defensive."

"I think you *can* be defensive," she said. "But not in the van. Yes, they weren't intentionally insulting you. They thought they were being respectful. They were just ignorant... and maybe kind of insulting. It's like when people in our town found out I grew up in the orphanage. They acted like I was Little Orphan Annie and made all these weird assumptions about how I lived. I'd tell them it was like boarding school, except I didn't go home for the holidays. They never believed me. They were sure I was scrubbing floors all day and sleeping in a lice-infested room with twenty other girls."

He nodded slowly. "You're right. It's like that, and I didn't mean to…" He trailed off and rubbed a hand over his face. "I was upset about the pot and about us not getting a better ride and knowing it was my fault, that if you'd been alone, you wouldn't have had to go through that."

"No, I just get picked up by random perverts."

A wan smile. "True. And honestly, I'd be lying if I said I wouldn't have acted that way otherwise. My parents taught me to be more polite. To accept that most people don't mean to be insulting, and to use that as a teaching opportunity. To gently relieve them of their misconceptions. It's just…it really bothers me, and unless I'm in a good mood, I get snippy."

"I don't blame you." She watched a couple of cars pass, then said, "Does that happen a lot? I guess it must, living in the suburbs and going to a private school." She realized how that sounded and hurried on. "I don't mean that Métis kids don't normally do that, just that they're a minority, and any minority—"

"You don't need to explain, Tess. I'm not going to jump down your throat." He raked his hair back. "And I guess I have jumped down your throat a few times, so I can't blame you. But you're right. It wouldn't matter what kind of minority you are, suburbs and private schools are mostly white kids. I've lived in the same neighborhood all my life. Went to the same school all my life. If anything, I'm sheltered there. Then I get out in the real world, and it's like with the *boulanger*—I don't know if he's being a jerk because I'm a teenage boy or a stranger or Métis. I've gotten more sensitive in the last year because..." He shrugged and went quiet.

Tess thought that was the end of the conversation, but then he cleared his throat and said, "I need to tell you something before we get to Montreal."

"All right."

"Earlier, I was getting on your case about being honest, and this is going to sound like something I should have mentioned sooner, but we were caught up in the journal, and I figured I'd tell you on the way and then..."

"You got caught up in the journal again."

"Yeah. Well, remember you asked about school? Whether I graduated?"

She nodded.

"I did. A year ago. I'm heading into my second year at McGill."

"Oh."

He shifted on the bench. "I wasn't being dishonest, but I wasn't rushing to tell you the truth either."

"You said you're almost eighteen. When's your birthday?"

"December."

She gave him a look. "It's June now. When I say I'm almost seventeen, I mean my birthday is next month. You're only six months older than me."

"Seven."

Another hard look. He sighed and shifted again. "All right. I didn't lie, but I may have misrepresented the truth.

I skipped a year. I don't go around announcing it. People act weird when they know you're smart."

"I think as soon as you open your mouth people know you're smart."

More fidgeting. "Anyway, my point was that if I'm sensitive about the minority thing, it's been...different this year. Being at university. Out of my usual environment." He rubbed a hand over his face. "I'm blathering. Sorry. Kind of tired. I'll stop talking now."

"I like it when you talk."

As soon as she said the words, her cheeks flamed red hot. She struggled for a way to fix it, to keep him from pulling back, withdrawing. But he gave her that wry smile again and said, "I think you're the first person who's ever said that."

"You have interesting things to say."

A sheepish nod. "Thanks."

"About McGill," she hurried on, feeling an awkward silence threatening. "What's it like? Being in university?"

He relaxed at that, and they talked about school until the bus came and continued talking as they boarded.

∽

Back to Montreal. Her first time through, Tess had felt overwhelmed—by the visions, the journey, the city—and it had been like ducking her head to run through a thunderstorm. She'd noticed little of her surroundings. Now, having made progress and feeling confident, with someone at her side to help her through the rough patches, she was in the mood to enjoy all the city had to offer. Unfortunately, Jackson wasn't.

They'd spent most of the bus trip chatting, and now he seemed talked out, in no mood to play tourist, let alone tour guide. She didn't even get to enjoy the sights from the window of an electric bus. At the bus station, he insisted on paying for a cab and directed the driver to take them straight to McGill.

At least the university was pretty. The campus was downtown, with exactly the sort of sprawling old buildings Tess had imagined a university should have. Green lawns rolled out in front like welcome mats. Summer students played Frisbee and read under massive old trees. Mount Royal—the mountain the city took its name from—loomed behind the campus.

Tess's feelings about university had always been mixed. She'd seen the allure of a higher education, but the allure of the greater world had pulled harder. Now, seeing the campus and the students, for perhaps the first time in her life she could imagine herself there. That set her stomach twisting a little. She'd always known exactly what she wanted: to get away from Hope, to explore and travel. Only two days out, though, and the world seemed to have shifted on its axis, throwing her off balance. There were choices. So many choices. Perhaps she'd been so intent on escape that she hadn't really considered them. It was an unsettling thought for a girl who prided herself on knowing what she wanted from life.

"What are we doing first?" Tess asked as the taxi dodged through traffic.

"Getting a room."

The driver understood enough English to look sharply at them through the rearview mirror.

"Getting separate dorm rooms for the night," Jackson clarified. "There are ones we can rent for a few days."

"It's only four o'clock," she said, then quickly added, "You're tired."

He made a noise in his throat that bordered on agreement. "It's summer term too. By the time we get settled, it'll be too late to find anyone in the psychology or psychiatry department. Also, the library closes soon."

"That's it then? We're in for the night?"

He nodded, then added a conciliatory, "We'll get an early start in the morning."

Tess tried not to show her disappointment. Everything he said might have been true, but she couldn't help feeling he was simply done for the day. Done talking. Done being companionable. Done with her. Which stung, but she could hardly blame him, given that he'd been woken last night by her screams and gotten little rest since. If she was being honest, she was exhausted too. The dorm promised a shower and hot food, and she was close enough to downtown to buy postcards and call Billy. A full evening.

"I'll keep reading the journal," he said. "I'll tell you what I find over breakfast."

Twenty-Three

ONCE WITHIN THE walls of McGill, she heard almost exclusively English, which seemed odd to her ear now, and while it made communication easier, she found herself wishing for the opportunity to exercise her French.

She was in a dorm just for girls. She had no idea if they were all divided that way, but that's where Jackson had put her. Once he had left, she'd called Billy and talked for as long as her change lasted. She'd told him about the house and the journal and that she was at McGill, following up. He was, perhaps, the one person who could hear that and say, "Cool," not "Are you nuts? You can't investigate by yourself."

Of course, she wasn't doing it by herself, but that was the part she excised from her account. The truth would sound ridiculous—that she'd met a backpacking student camping out in an abandoned house, hired him and they were now at McGill, solving her mystery together. Billy would react in the same way Jackson had to Steve. Did she really think

Jackson was helping her out of the goodness of his heart? Well, no. The idea made her laugh. He was helping because this mystery promised far more excitement than hitch-hiking through the Quebec countryside. But to understand that, you needed to know Jackson, and Billy did not.

Having bought postcards nearby, along with snacks and a notebook, she spent most of the evening writing to her friends. One distinct advantage of the postcard form: there wasn't room for more than a few lines, meaning no one would expect details of her adventure. A simple: *Salut de Montreal! Still hard at work, unraveling the mystery of my past while improving my deplorable French (remember how Mlle. Béringer said we'd be all set for Paris? We aren't!) Hope you are making progress of your own. Miss you! XOXO Tess*

She then found a mini-library in the dorm common room, where guests had left behind books for others. She took *The Collector*, which she'd seen on a new-release shelf in the train station. She got about fifty pages in before realizing it was, quite possibly, the worst book she could have picked to read at the moment. It was the story of a girl "collected" by a predator, who locked her in a room like his precious butterflies. She put it aside quickly but still spent the night surfing through dreams where Steve took her captive and trapped her in one of the mansion's closets.

Despite her nightmares, she awoke feeling refreshed. Or perhaps simply relieved that the night was over. At just past seven, she was bounding down the front steps, showered and dressed in her boots, scarf and a miniskirt she'd found among the clothes Billy gave her. She even had a newly purchased notebook under her arm and a fountain pen in her pocket, and she felt like an actual university student. When she came down the steps, a boy going up swiveled to watch her, and she grinned at him.

"Thérèse."

Jackson sat on the balustrade that enclosed the front porch. He checked his watch as she walked over.

"You said seven thirty at the cafeteria, didn't you?"

He grunted and eyed her as she swung over to him.

"You're chipper this morning." His tone suggested he took this as a personal affront.

"And you are not. You didn't stay up all right reading that journal, I hope."

Another grunt.

"You look as if you did," she said. "At least you seem to have showered, though, which is an improvement."

She grinned as she said it. Teasing him, and perhaps, yes, needling him a little, which she'd learned was more likely to shake his ill temper than solicitude.

"Yeah, yeah," he muttered. "Are you going to be able to sit still through breakfast?"

"Of course. I may skip all the way there though. That won't embarrass you, will it?"

"We're not going to the caf." He lifted a bag from his side. A bakery bag, the smell of fresh bread wafting out. "The library opens at eight, and I want to be there when it does."

"Yes, sir."

They crossed the lawn and found a place not yet shaded, the morning cool and the sun warm.

"I finished the journal," he said as they started eating. "I made notes."

He passed her a sheaf of papers. At least ten of them, in single-spaced, perfect handwriting.

"You *were* up all night," she said. "You shouldn't have—"

"I was in bed before midnight. Now, about the journal. I've determined they were doing sensory-deprivation experiments."

"Sensory...?"

"Depriving someone of sensory input. Sight, sound, touch, taste, smell. Normally, it's done with a hood or a tank. The purpose is to induce a meditative state and allow the subject to focus."

She stared at him. "Meditative state? Those boxes—"

"I know. Clearly, whoever was in them was not relaxing and enjoying a quiet rest. What I'm saying is that sensory deprivation has been used in psychiatry, and it's not considered cruel in small amounts. But the system normally used is humane. Like a tank filled with salt water. Not a wooden casket."

"The journal says that's why they were using those?"

"It alludes to that. I can't figure out exactly what they were hoping to accomplish, but it seems, as you saw, that the doctor who wrote the journal became increasingly disillusioned with the work and increasingly concerned for the patients. He began to suspect that he'd been sold a bill of goods."

"What?"

"That the purpose of the research had been misrepresented to him."

"What did he think they were really doing?"

"He never says. Even though he was hiding the journal, he was still cagey. No names. No specifics. His concerns are generalizations. As for the supposed treatment, I've compiled his oblique references on this page"—he pulled one out—"and my theory is that they were treating depression by inducing a relaxed state with drugs and then putting the patient in the boxes. The closet seems to have been an early stage of the experiment—without drugs—followed by the wooden boxes. Yet while the subjects were all volunteers, not all of them could voluntarily withstand the experience. Some panicked despite the sedative."

"That primal fear," she said. "Claustrophobia."

"Correct. That is where the author began questioning the ethics and purpose of the research. Subjects who objected weren't permitted another method of treatment."

"Or allowed to leave."

Jackson fingered the journal pages. "There's no proof of that. I'm not defending what they did, Tess, but I don't like jumping to conclusions that these men were—"

"Evil?"

"Exactly. They were scientists. Yes, maybe subjects *were* held against their will if they objected, but I don't want to presume that without evidence. Psychiatrists are supposed to abide by the Nuremberg Code when they do human experimentation. The first principle is that subjects must be able to consent and do so voluntarily, under no duress."

"All right."

He seemed to visibly relax at that, as if he'd expected her to argue. He was right though. It was easy to see whatever had happened in that house as something straight out of a gothic novel. Mad scientists experimenting on unwitting patients. Without proof, though, they could travel too far down the wrong road and miss a simple answer while looking for a nefarious one.

"I called my mom last night," he said. "Asked if she knew of any link between McGill and sensory-deprivation research."

"What did you tell her?"

He seemed confused by the question before saying, "Nothing. I just asked." For him, it seemed, that was normal. Raised to ask questions and explore whatever piqued his curiosity. Which explained a lot, and Tess couldn't help feeling a twinge of envy.

"She knew of a connection," he said. "Donald Hebb. He's a psychology professor at McGill. Chairman of the department until '59, and then he served as president of the American Psychological Association in 1960."

"Wow."

"Yes, he's a big deal in the field. He's still here, teaching, though my mom's not sure what his position is.

She remembers, though, that he was known for sensory-deprivation experiments, because she heard him speak on it a few years ago. He studied its effects on the mind. What he found suggested the effects weren't positive. My mom doesn't know much more, but we should be able to dig deeper here."

"Hebb, you said? Is he mentioned in the journal? I know there's a Dr. K. mentioned."

"And a Dr. H., which I'm guessing is Hebb. However, Dr. H. didn't seem to have anything to do with the actual experiments. He's cited because of research he did on the subject, and there are a few passages that suggest Dr. K. was a student of his—either literally, by taking his classes, or figuratively, by studying his work. Nothing suggests Hebb was in any way involved with what happened in Sainte-Suzanne. In fact, at one point the journal writer says he told Dr. K. that he's misusing Dr. H.'s research and that if the man found out, he'd be horrified."

"They were taking Hebb's research a step further."

"Seems so. Now we need to find out what Hebb's research was."

ꝅ

After a couple of hours at the library, they had their answers. While at Harvard, Donald Hebb had studied the effects of sensory deprivation on rats. Then, in 1951, the Canadian Defense Research Board paid him to start human trials.

He'd given McGill students a lot of money—twenty dollars a day—to volunteer. They were placed on beds in a cell-like room and fitted with goggles to block out light and earphones to block out sound. Tubes over their arms and gloves on their hands ensured they couldn't feel anything.

The tests were conducted as humanely as possible. Participants ate and used the washroom—still wearing goggles and headphones. They were allowed to quit at any time.

The trial was supposed to last six weeks. Most subjects gave up after a few days. Only one made it a full week.

Hebb had theorized that without sensory stimulation, cognitive abilities would deteriorate. He was right. All the subjects performed poorly on tests afterward. Instead of allowing them to focus, prolonged deprivation actually made them confused, easily misled. Some even reported visual and auditory hallucinations.

The purpose of the experiments had been more than mere academic interest. The defense department feared the Soviets had used sensory deprivation to brainwash Canadian POWs.

Whatever happened at the house near Sainte-Suzanne, it had stemmed from this research. Yet if Hebb had found negative effects from sensory deprivation, why would anyone use it to *cure* mentally ill patients?

A possible answer came in an article's reference to another McGill professor: Dr. Ewen Cameron, who'd been head of the psychiatry department while Hebb headed psychology. Cameron had used Hebb's work to "reprogram" mentally ill patients with a combination of isolation, drugs and hypnosis.

"Is that what we were seeing?" Tess asked. "Cameron's work?"

"I don't think so. His work started in the mid-'50s, which means it's past the date you saw on that calendar. But I know where we might get more information. Cameron's still doing work here, over at Ravenscrag."

Twenty-Four

RAVENSCRAG. THESE DAYS it was more
commonly called the Allan Memorial Institute. Ravenscrag
fit it better. The mansion outside Sainte-Suzanne paled in
comparison to this. Built a hundred years ago as a family home,
it had been the biggest and grandest mansion in Canada.
Donated to the university twenty-five years ago, it was now
home to Royal Victoria Hospital's psychiatry department.

Jackson went straight to the departmental secretary
and asked after Dr. Cameron. He introduced himself and
showed his student card, and Tess wondered why he did
that until the secretary recognized his name. She knew his
mother, who apparently gave lectures at McGill.

When they'd first asked about Dr. Cameron, the secretary's face had gone rigid, and Tess had been certain they'd
get a flat no. After realizing who Jackson was, her answer was
still no, but only because Dr. Cameron was home in Albany.

Jackson explained that he and Tess were doing a summer project on sensory deprivation. He'd read the basics of Cameron's work, but they hadn't been able to find more in the library.

"I'm not surprised," the secretary said. "As far as I know, he hasn't published his findings yet. But there's a research assistant here who works with him. He's in his office now if you'd like me to ring him."

"Please."

The secretary did that and then led them back. A young man stood in an office doorway, looking annoyed. He ushered them in brusquely and closed the door without a word to the secretary.

While the assistant sat on the edge of his desk, he clearly expected them to stand.

"Jackson Labine." Jackson walked forward, hand out. "My mother is—"

"I've heard. I'm not familiar with her work. I'm quite busy, as you can see, and I don't appreciate being interrupted by a couple of high-school students trading on some psychologist's name to weasel their way in here."

He said *psychologist* the way a surgeon might say *veterinarian*, as if any link between their professions was unappreciated.

"I'm a McGill student," Jackson said evenly as he withdrew his card. "I'm going into my second year. This is a summer research project."

"You bring your high-school girlfriend along on interviews? That's not very professional."

"She's an intern of my mother's, and I am paying her to assist me in this project."

Tess opened her notebook and took out her pen.

The man waved at her. "You can put that away. I don't have anything to say." He looked at Jackson. "Did you really think that would work? Pretending you're doing *research* for a *project?*"

"I am. I—"

"Yes, I suppose technically you are. It's the nature of the project you're lying about, isn't it?"

"What—"

"Did your mother think this would work better? Sending her son to gather dirt? Whatever she's heard about Dr. Cameron's work, it's slander, started by those jealous of his success, and if she spreads those lies, she will be charged with libel, and the case will be tight enough that your father won't be able to get her off."

"I thought you didn't know my mother."

"I said I don't know her work. Her *psychology* work. Because that's what she is. A psychologist. If she was a halfway decent one, that's what she'd be recognized for. But she can't make a name for herself that way, so she sticks her nose where it doesn't belong. Your being here obviously means she has Dr. Cameron in her sights."

"Obviously ," Jackson murmured.

"I suppose the fact that it took her so long should prove she's not much of a threat. His work here is done. His project is old news."

"If the truth hasn't been exposed, it's still news."

Jackson's gaze was fixed on the man. A knowing smile played on his lips. Tess was sure his mother had no interest in Dr. Cameron, but if the assistant had leaped to that conclusion, Jackson seemed happy to play along.

The man leaned forward. "I'm going to warn both of you to back off. The American government doesn't appreciate having its reputation besmirched, and the CIA is one division you really don't want to upset."

"Considering I'm not in America, I'm not too worried. Maybe *our* government would like to know that the CIA is involved with Dr. Cameron's work."

"They're not. That's the point I'm making. The rumor is a lie, one the CIA does not appreciate, so tell your mother—"

"My mother's sole concern is for the patients involved. What you've done to them."

The man tensed, and Jackson couldn't hide a small smile of satisfaction. Tess realized his remark about the patients had been a blind stab.

The man recovered fast. "The patients are fine. Better than fine. They are improved. That was the point of the experiment, and it has been a rousing success—"

"*Rousing?* Perhaps that word doesn't mean what you think it does. You seem to be a native English speaker."

"I know what the word means, boy." The man's face mottled bright red. "The experiment was an *overwhelming success.*"

"That's not what some of the patients are claiming."

A harsh laugh. "If your mother honestly thinks *all* patients are pleased with their treatment, that shows exactly how inept she is at her profession. We're dealing with the mentally ill here. They're troubled. Sometimes we can't cure them, and they blame us. Sometimes we *do* cure them, and they still blame us. I've seen violent schizophrenics put on medication that allows them to lead a normal life then complain because the meds give them the shakes."

"True, but as psychiatrists, you're medical doctors. *First do no harm.*"

The man's face mottled darker. "We have done no harm. The memory loss is temporary. It was an anticipated effect of the coma induction."

"Which was better than Dr. Hebb's methods of sensory deprivation?"

The man waved his hands. "It's not exactly the same thing, but yes, on the most simplistic layman's level, it was more humane to induce comas to reprogram the brain, which comes with the risk of short-term amnesia. Anyone who is suggesting more permanent effects is fear-mongering. And that is all I'm going to say. You can leave on your own or escorted by security."

As they headed out, Jackson continued to pester the research assistant with questions.

"I'm going to find the washroom," Tess said.

The man waved her off. He might have been pointing to the facilities...or he might have just been telling her to go away. She walked to the end of the hall and turned. Down another hall and another.

No sign of a washroom, but she wasn't actually looking for one. She had no idea what she hoped to find. She just kept walking, as if she followed some invisible map. Turn here and here and then here. Finally, she reached what seemed to be a medical area. Peeking through one window, she saw an examination table. When she heard voices, she ducked behind the corner.

She peeked out to see a man leading a hospital-gowned woman toward her. Another man accompanied them. The first man's face grabbed her attention. It was the research assistant she'd just left.

He couldn't possibly have escorted Jackson out and then retrieved a patient in so short a time. Tess peeked again and got a better look at the older man with him. She'd noticed his photo in the front hall. It was Dr. Ewen Cameron.

She was seeing a vision.

Tess weighed the risks of her being mistaken and decided they were worth taking. She stepped from behind the corner, walked into the middle of the hall and stood there. The trio kept coming. There was no way they could miss seeing her, yet they gave no sign that they did.

The younger man seemed to be reassuring the woman. As he'd demonstrated in his office, he wasn't really suited for such a conversation, and the patient grew more agitated as he spoke. Dr. Cameron moved closer. "Depression is not uncommon after a pregnancy," he said, his voice soft, with a Scottish burr. "But this is the worst possible time for it. Your children need you. We're going to give you back to them. That's what you want, isn't it?"

The woman replied in rapid-fire French, and Tess could only pick up something about sleeping and shocks. The doctor patted her shoulder. "All part of the process. Unpleasant, but you're a strong woman. You'll get through this and get back to your wee ones in no time."

Dr. Cameron opened a door, and the three disappeared into a room. Tess hurried over and grabbed the closing door, but it kept shutting. She put her ear to it.

"*Que faites-vous là?*" What are you doing there? A woman's voice came from down the hall. Tess blinked, and when she did, a sign appeared on the door, in French and English, saying the laboratory was closed. A woman in a lab coat strode her way.

"I—I'm looking for the washroom," Tess said in English.

"Well, that's not it. This is a restricted area."

"Sorry, I was in the psychiatry department, and I took a wrong turn. Can you point me back toward reception? That's where my friend's waiting."

The woman insisted on walking her out.

Twenty-Five

ONCE TESS AND Jackson were outside, she told him what she'd seen.

"I don't know what she meant about shocks," Tess said. "Maybe I translated wrong."

"No, it's electroshock therapy. Common enough."

"Shocking people? Therapeutically?"

"It's been shown to have positive effects. Negative ones too though. My mother is part of a group of psychologists who advocate against it because—" He made a face. "Avoid tangent. Stay on track. What you saw is significant because it proves—"

A group of laughing students drowned him out, and he plucked her sleeve, impatiently leading her across the road to quiet. "I was still talking to the guy when you saw him. I kept asking him questions. So he's not dead."

"Um, no. Unless we're both seeing ghosts."

"Neither of us is. *That's* the point."

"Right," she said slowly. "If I saw someone that we know is definitely alive, then I can't be seeing ghosts. They're replays of the past."

"Which reminds me that we wanted to speak to someone about that. We'll go see if he's around."

⌒

The professor's name was Dr. Augustin, and he was in the psychology building, doing research through the summer term. He was a large man in his sixties, with a ruddy complexion and a bristling gray mustache. He greeted Jackson warmly, asking after his parents and sisters as he led them to his office. Jackson asked if his research was going well.

"Well enough," Dr. Augustin said in heavily accented English. "We are doing a standard ESP test with psy-Q forms before and after." He looked at Tess. "That means we ask questions about subjects' perceived psychic abilities, run an ESP test and then re-question them about their abilities afterward."

"Seeing whether success or failure on the test influences their answers," Jackson said.

"Correct, but we also have a second group that is *not* told how well they did. They guess at their score and then take the questionnaires, testing how perception affects their responses. It is just the first step in an array of escalating tests, ultimately looking at the effects of perceived psychic abilities." He smiled as he opened his door. "Which is not what you came to see me about."

"It's still interesting," Tess said.

"Not really, but *merci, mademoiselle*." Another smile, self-deprecating but pleased too, proud of his work.

They settled into Dr. Augustin's office. On the walls were framed newspaper clippings. Some were about psychics who'd used their powers to find missing people and solve crimes. Others were about hypnosis, using it on witnesses to do the same.

"Thérèse, is it?" he said. "I notice Jackson uses the French pronunciation, but you seem to be an English speaker."

"I'm from Ontario but originally French. Well, I think so. I'm tracking down my roots."

"Ah. Your parents let you travel so far afield at your age? How old are you? Seventeen?"

"Almost. As for my parents, that's what I'm looking for. I was raised in an orphanage."

"Really?" His brows shot up. "I did not know such things still existed. I suppose they must, but…" He shook his head. "They should not. There are so many people who wish children but cannot have them. Raised in an orphanage with no idea who you are? It sounds like some-thing out of a Dickens novel."

She smiled. "It wasn't as bad as that."

"Oh, I know. This is not Dickens's London, *Dieu merci*. Forgive me for prying, mademoiselle. As Jackson can tell you,

I am a terribly nosy old man. Too much time in laboratories and libraries. The lives of others hold endless fascination."

"Everyone's life is interesting, if it's different from your own."

A broader smile creased his wide face. "Very true. And you are most gracious to forgive my interest, but I will turn my attention to your original purpose in coming to see me, before Jackson explodes from impatience."

Jackson murmured an apology. The old man only laughed and told him to go on.

"We're interested in psychic phenomena," Jackson said. "A specific manifestation that may or may not be a recognized type."

"Now that is intriguing." Dr. Augustin leaned toward Tess. "Dare I hope that you yourself are the one who has experienced it?"

"No, sorry," she said and went on to tell the story they'd agreed on—that it was a fellow orphan, and since they were at McGill, Jackson had suggested they ask Dr. Augustin about it.

She started by describing the figures she saw in the present day.

"They aren't ghosts," she said. "My friend can't communicate with them, and they make no attempt to communicate with her. They're just going about their lives."

"That does not mean they are not ghosts. While it seems your friend is hoping for a more unique explanation, I fear that would be my first guess."

"There's more," Jackson said.

Tess explained the other visions—the ones where "her friend" seemed to shift into the past. As she spoke, the professor's eyes widened.

"Retrocognition," he said. "*Oui*, of course. That would explain the spectral figures as well. They do not seem alarmed or confused by being in the present day because they are not. It is as if a tiny window opens between past and present, and they cross over. Their image crosses over, that is. Rather like a projector playing an old movie."

"I don't understand," Tess said.

"Forgive me, mademoiselle. I am rushing on. This is exciting. It is a rare phenomenon, as psychic experiences go. As Jackson may have told you, I am not truly a believer. I merely study it. There are, however, some alleged manifestations that I find more possible than others. Retrocognition is one of them. More commonly, people claim to have precognition—they see the future. I do not believe that is possible. I certainly hope our lives cannot be laid out on such a definitive path. But retrocognition, as the name implies, means seeing the past, often by stepping into another time altogether."

He stood and pulled a book from the shelf. "I have the most famous account of it here." He laid the book in front of her, opened to a page talking about something called the Moberly–Jourdain incident, when two young women had visited the Palace of Versailles and somehow found themselves back in the time of Marie Antoinette.

"When your friend passes into another period, does she ever find herself in a different place?"

Tess shook her head. "It's the same place where she is. It's just another time."

"That is usually the case with retrocognition. In fact, if the person claims to step into another location, it is widely believed to be a sign that the answer is more likely an active imagination than psychic abilities." He lowered himself back into his chair. "I do not suppose there is a chance I could speak to your friend? I could certainly bring her here—pay her train ticket and boarding. As I said, retrocognition is extremely rare. I would very much like to speak to her."

Jackson glanced at her, and Tess could tell he wanted her to admit it wasn't a friend. Yes, it would be nice to talk to someone like Dr. Augustin, who would take her seriously. But she suspected Dr. Augustin wasn't going anywhere soon. No need to rush.

She said that she'd speak to her friend and then sneaked a look at Jackson, but he only gave a small nod.

"There's one other thing," Jackson said. "It's department-mental, rather than specific to your studies. I'm interested in Dr. Hebb's work. The sensory-deprivation experiments in particular. The subject came up in my psych class last year, and it intrigued me."

It did not intrigue Dr. Augustin. Tess could see that by the flash of disappointment.

"Of course, I know Donald," Dr. Augustin said. "He is a wonderful man, and one of Canada's greatest contributors to the field of psychology. I will admit, though, that I find the sensory-deprivation work distasteful."

"Because of the military connections?" Jackson asked.

"*Oui*. I understand in Donald's case the military claimed to be exploring a concern about brainwashing, but I cannot help but fear..."

"They were looking for methods they could use themselves?"

"*Oui*, but as you know, I am something of a..." A brief but warm smile. "What does your mother call it? Conspiracy nut?"

"She means it in the most affectionate way."

Dr. Augustin laughed. "She has many of us in her social circle, so I take no offense."

"On that topic then, can you tell me anything about Dr. Ewen Cameron?"

"That is psychiatry. I am not much involved with the research or politics of that department."

"Dr. Cameron is apparently doing research based on Dr. Hebb's."

Dr. Augustin couldn't disguise a brief grimace of distaste. "Then that would explain why I do not know his work, despite his illustrious reputation."

"Not even if it's rumored to be funded by the CIA?"

Dr. Augustin's head shot up at that, and Jackson laughed. The professor waved a finger at him. "You are as bad as your *maman*, do you know that?"

"I thought it might catch your interest. Nothing then?"

"*Non*, and now I will have to investigate, drawing my attention away from my studies. As my Anglophone students would say, thanks for nothing."

Jackson grinned. "Sorry. If you do investigate and find anything, Tess and I are staying on campus." He named the dorms. "We'll be here for a few more days. After that you can always reach me through my mother. I touch base every day or two."

"As a good son should. Your *maman* likes to give her children their freedom, but she does worry. We were speaking just the other day and she told me you were off on this journey of discovery."

Jackson tensed but only said, "*D'accord*. I will call her later and tell her I saw you. She'll like that. Now, Tess and I should leave you to—"

"Are you having any luck with your investigations?" Dr. Augustin asked.

"Yes, quite a bit, actually." Jackson motioned for Tess to rise, and when she wasn't quick enough, he took hold of her sleeve and tugged her up. "It's been very productive, but we should get back to it and leave you to your own—"

"I presume there is a connection then?" he said. "Between your birth parents and Thérèse's?"

Tess turned a slow look on Jackson, but he ducked it and prodded her toward the hall, mumbling some nonanswer. He practically shoved her out the door and almost closed it between them as he spoke to Dr. Augustin in rapid-fire French. As fast as he talked, though, she could pick up enough to know that he was saying goodbye and thanking Dr. Augustin for his help...while briefly answering Dr. Augustin's queries about this other investigation, the one that apparently involved his parents. His *birth* parents. Tess listened until she'd heard enough. Then she strode down the hall.

A moment later she heard, "Tess?" Then "Tess!" and running footsteps behind her. She picked up her pace and kept going.

Twenty-Six

"**TESS!**" **JACKSON CALLED** as she strode out of the building. "Hold on! I can explain."

"Of course you can," she said as he caught up. "I'm sure you will. However, it's about two days and twelve hours too late."

"It's not like that."

"No?" She turned to face him. "All right. What you're telling me is that you happen to be searching for your birth parents at the same time I am, and we happened to end up in the same place. Yet that's a total coincidence, and therefore there was no reason to tell me."

"I—"

"Furthermore, given that the two are unconnected, you are helping me out of simple curiosity, and you certainly never agreed to help me—and take my money—only because my search might actually provide answers for yours."

He rubbed his mouth and looked around. "Can we go somewhere and talk? Please?"

"That's what I was trying to do, presuming you didn't want to have this conversation in the middle of the psychology department."

He nodded and gestured for her to follow him. She did, and they wound past a few buildings before coming to a bench between two of them.

They sat. When Jackson didn't speak, she said, "Start at the beginning. The part where your parents aren't your birth parents, which would be none of my business normally but obviously is, under the circumstances."

"They're my aunt and uncle," he said. "Dad is my birth mother's older brother. That's what I think of them as: Mom and Dad. I've never known my birth parents. I didn't even realize they existed until I was old enough for my parents to explain. That's why my sisters are so much older. When my birth mother was a teen, she got into some trouble. Dad stepped in to help. She had…issues. Psychological. He got her on the right path, and then she met my birth father and wanted to drop out of school and get married. She was seventeen. When my parents tried to change her mind, she took off. She got married and had me, and they never even knew I existed until my birth father showed up on their doorstep with me, six months old, and said she was dead."

Tess blinked, the words *I'm sorry* on her lips, but he continued.

"She'd had postpartum depression, like that woman you saw in the hall. She'd always had problems with depression, and having me only made it worse."

He was leaning forward, gazing straight ahead, some piece of paper—it looked like Dr. Augustin's card—between his hands, nails shredding the edges as he spoke.

"She...committed suicide. Pills. My birth father was a mess. My parents say he really did love her, but he was just a kid himself, and he didn't understand her problems. He thought he could fix them by being good to her. Loving her. Looking after her." The breeze caught a tiny scrap of the card and floated it away. "That's not enough. It just isn't. He brought me to my parents and asked them to take me until he got on his feet again. He'd heard of work in Newfoundland at the fisheries. He'd make some money and come back. He died on the way out there. Drove all day and then decided he could drive the rest of the way that night. He fell asleep at the wheel."

"I'm sorry."

He gave a half shrug. "I don't know them as anything more than photos. It's like a really tragic story that happened to someone else, you know? A story about two kids who weren't much older than I am now, who only wanted to get married and be happy like everyone else, and it went really, really wrong."

"Your mother," Tess said. "You think that house, that experiment, has something to do with her depression...but there's no way you could coincidentally happen to be in the same house, on the same mission, when I showed up."

He turned toward her. "There's this man. He contacted me when I started at McGill. It was a letter at first, to my dorm room. He wanted to talk to me about my birth mother. If I agreed, I was to wait by a pay phone the next day at a certain time."

She raised her brows.

"Yes, I know it sounds very cloak-and-dagger," he said.

"Mysterious man contacts you to set up mysterious meeting via pay phone? No, not at all strange."

"It's true, Tess. I swear it."

"Just tell me your story."

"I went to the pay phone. He called. He said there was more to my mother's story than I knew. I asked him what he meant. He said he didn't know the specifics, only that the situation was much more complicated than postpartum depression and suicide. I demanded more. He said I'd need to get answers myself. I hung up. I had no idea what was going on, but it seemed like someone was just trying to cause trouble. It seemed too weird to be legitimate. That's why I freaked out when you said you were sent to the same place. It seemed like proof I'd been set up, though I had no idea why."

"But you *did* eventually talk to the guy again?"

"He continued to send messages to my dorm. I ignored him for almost six months. Then I took one of his calls. By then I hoped that if he really had anything to tell me, he'd tell me and stop playing games."

"Did he?"

"Not really. He said he knew that my mother had been involved in something. He had no idea what it was, but he could set me on my way if I was interested in investigating.

I needed more. Where did this information come from? *What* was the information, so I could judge it for myself? This time he hung up on me. Then last week he called my parents' place. I was home by then, the term over. He gave me the address for the house outside Sainte-Suzanne. He said if I wanted answers, they would be there in a day or two."

"Because I was going there? You must think I really am stupid, Jackson. There's no way this man could have known I was heading to that house. The only person who did was—"

"Whoever gave you that address. She must have called and told him."

Tess shook her head. "If the matron knew of someone who could help, she would have told me."

"Maybe he didn't know you were definitely going, only that you'd gotten the address somehow."

"That's awfully..." She trailed off. "When did he call?"

"Sunday afternoon."

"I tried the Sainte-Suzanne number that day," Tess said. "When the operator said it wasn't in service, the matron spoke to her and explained a bit about the situation."

Jackson nodded. "Then it was the local operator. I bet she'd been told to call this man if anyone used that number. He knew you'd get that number when you turned eighteen, and if I wouldn't investigate, maybe you would. Then you called it early, and he used that excuse to send me up there. At least one of us would take the bait. While I don't like doing the bidding of some mysterious guy too lazy to get off his ass and do it himself, there are answers here, answers we both need.

I think we made some real progress today." He pulled out his notepad. "Let's compile what we've found and—"

"No."

He went still, notebook half open, other hand reaching for his pen.

"Do you really think it's that easy, Jackson?"

His jaw twitched, as if to say, *No, but I'd kinda hoped it might be.*

"Look, Tess, I know you're upset with me. Maybe I didn't handle this well—"

"Maybe? There's no maybe about it. You were a jerk."

He flinched hard at that. "I don't think—"

"No? You hauled me out of that basement, blamed me for inconveniencing you and kicked me out to sleep in the woods. The next morning, I offered to hire you, and you took my money—to do exactly what you'd come there to do anyway."

"I hadn't figured out what was going on, if you were on the level or if that man had sent you up there, so I decided to pretend—"

"You lied to me," she said. "How many times did you tell me that if you were going to help, I had to be honest. How many times did you make me feel bad for not being completely honest?"

"I—"

"You were a jerk, Jackson."

"Okay, I've been thoughtless. Inconsiderate. I know I can *act* like a jerk, but I think I let you see beyond that."

"You let me see a lie."

He rubbed his mouth again, his gaze focused forward, distant. Then he turned to her. "The story I told was a lie, but what you've seen—"

"What you've *let* me see, as you worded it yourself. That small, safe window you allowed me to peek in, mostly as a way to make me feel like I knew you, so we could work together. Don't try to make me feel special because you let me in. I'm not special. I'm just the sucker who fell for your lies."

"That's not—"

"I *paid* you. I gave you five dollars to help me. I bought all the food you needed. I even got your bus ticket. And you let me, despite the fact—"

"It was temporary. Part of me playing a role." He fumbled for his wallet and pulled out a twenty. "There. That'll more than cover it, and you can keep the extra."

"Can I? Thank you."

He missed the sarcasm and nodded. "I can give you more if you need it. I have more than enough."

"From Daddy and Mommy?"

His gaze dropped slightly, and he mumbled, "I do stuff for them. Research and that. I earn it. Okay, I get more than I earn, but I'm in school, and they want me to concentrate on my studies." He sneaked a look at her. "The point is that I have money. I can pay for everything from now on, and I can give you some extra if you need—"

"I *don't* need it."

"I know you must, so let me pay, as a way of saying I'm sorry."

"I'd rather you just said you were sorry."

"I am."

"Not really. You admit you may have made a mistake or two, but you still think I'm overreacting and money will fix it. When I say I don't need your money, Jackson, I mean it. I have plenty. Some came from the matron, but most I made myself, from years of doing whatever work I could find so that when I was ready to set out on my own, I could do it without relying on jerks who think they're better than me because Daddy and Mommy give them an allowance."

He exhaled. "You're right. I handled that poorly. I've handled a lot of things poorly, but I don't think—"

"You don't think you're a jerk. Maybe you aren't, but you're doing a fine imitation of one." She got to her feet. "I'm going to my dorm for a while."

When she started walking away, he leaped up behind her. "Tess! Don't go. I know I'm not saying the right things, but I don't know what I'm supposed to say."

"If you did know and you said that, then it would be more lies, wouldn't it? Telling me what I want to hear so I shut up. Do you know what I want to hear? Honesty."

"All right. I'm…I'm sorry?" His voice rose, turning it into a question. A sharp shake of his head. "I *am* sorry. You're right. I deceived you and then gave you crap for being less than honest about things that had nothing to do with me. What *I* lied about did affect you. So it's worse." A hopeful look. "Is that good?"

Tess sighed. "I'm not trying to force you to say the right things, Jackson. I just need a break—"

"No, you're taking off."

"Do you really think I'd abandon the investigation and reject your help because you hurt my feelings? I'm angry, Jackson. Justifiably angry, but this is what happens when you deal with strangers. They can deceive you. Lesson learned. I'm not going to run away, because I'm not stupid. I need a break to regroup, and then I want to get back into the investigation. You're useful to me; I'm useful to you. It's a business arrangement. That's all."

He stood there staring at her, looking confused and maybe a little bit hurt, as if he'd rather she stomped off because then he could just chase after her and apologize and...Tess didn't know what he expected then. That she'd fall into his arms and tell him it was all right, that he was a great guy after all? The idea almost made her snort a laugh, but there was something in his expression that said that's exactly what he hoped for. That he could get out of this because she wasn't really angry—he'd just hurt her feelings.

"May I go now?" she asked.

He nodded mutely.

"Meet me back here in two hours," she said as she walked away. "Bring your notes."

He let her get to the edge of the walkway, then called after her, "Tess!"

"It's Thérèse," she said and kept going.

Twenty-Seven

TESS ARRIVED BACK at the meeting place to find Jackson pacing, as if he expected she wouldn't show up. She was actually ten minutes early.

He'd bought maple taffy from the confectioner and a gothic novel he "just happened to see in a window." She took both without comment and squelched a pang of guilt. He'd gone out of his way to find things that might cheer her up. The problem was, given the way he'd talked earlier, she felt less flattered than manipulated, as if he thought her such a silly girl that candies and paperback novels would erase any ill will between them.

She moved the conversation directly onto the safer terrain of their investigation, and they spent the next couple of hours piecing together what they'd learned. They concluded that it seemed as if the work in Sainte-Suzanne might have been a step between Dr. Hebb's work and Dr. Cameron's experiments. Hebb had studied sensory deprivation as humanely as possible, with willing and mentally sound subjects. Cameron seemed to have used mentally ill subjects who, while still volunteers, would be less able to grant objective permission, and judging from the scene Tess had witnessed, there'd been psychological coercion involved.

The Sainte-Suzanne study used mental patients, primarily those suffering from depression. It employed methods of sensory deprivation much less humane than Hebb's, while adding sedatives in an attempt to counteract the negative impact. Compared to Hebb's—and presumably Cameron's—methods, the ones at Sainte-Suzanne seemed almost primitively brutal.

"Maybe they're supposed to be," Tess said as Jackson commented on that. "Primitive so they can be reproduced easily, outside a laboratory. Brutal because they're not intended to be used on willing subjects."

Jackson shook his head. "You can't do that, Te—Thérèse. Like I said, there are rules. Codes of ethics that apply to all research, and the only point of doing research is to test legal drugs or therapeutic methods or get published, meaning there's no point ducking the codes."

"What if the application is for someone who doesn't have any rights?"

"Everyone has rights."

"Even prisoners of war?"

He stopped and looked at her. Confused at first. Then excitement lit his gray eyes, and Tess's gut clenched with a pang of grief for something she'd had and lost.

She barely knew him. That's what she'd been telling herself, sitting in her dorm room for the last two hours. She'd met him three days ago. A passing acquaintance. If they'd parted ways after their fight, perhaps in a few years she would be unable to picture him. In a decade, she might have forgotten his name. Someday, if she came back to Montreal, she might think, I knew a boy here once, didn't I?

Except that wasn't true at all. She wouldn't forget what he looked like. Wouldn't forget his name. Wouldn't forget *him*. And that only made it so much worse. To meet someone who made an indelible impression and then lose him so quickly, realizing she'd never really known him at all, that he'd used her, she really wished she *could* forget he'd ever existed.

Tess swallowed, dropped her gaze and busied herself making a meaningless note in her book as she said casually, "It's a possibility then?"

"It's the missing piece, Tess. Hebb's work was funded by defense, ostensibly to study brainwashing because they feared what it did to their soldiers. And Cameron, who by his own admission was influenced by Hebb, seems to be working for the CIA. The CIA has been trying to perfect brainwashing for years. They fostered the large-scale production of LSD, and they led the expedition that discovered magic mushrooms. They thought those drugs were the key to manipulating behavior."

As he talked, his face lit up and his eyes glowed, and she saw again that brilliant, intense and complex boy.

At first glance dark and cold but, filled with tamped-down energy just waiting for a spark to ignite it, and then blazing so brightly she couldn't look away.

"We still have lots of work to do confirming this," he said. "But as a theory, it's perfect. Whoever was in charge at Sainte-Suzanne was building on Hebb's work in a less-than-ethical way. That's why the experiments weren't conducted here at McGill. No one would give permission to put mentally ill subjects in boxes, padded or not. But if you wanted a cheap and easily replicated method of inducing sensory deprivation, that works. Sedate the subjects enough that they don't struggle but not so much that they're unaware of their surroundings. Those scratches we saw and the voices you heard were the result of attempts to find the right dosage, which would vary with each patient."

He settled back, smiling now. "There we have it. A working theory. Thanks to you."

"The question then is, how does it connect to us? You said your mother suffered from postpartum depression. We know the house at Sainte-Suzanne opened before you were born and was still operating a couple of years afterward, so..."

She trailed off then, seeing his expression. The grin had fallen away, replaced by a dawning horror and then shame.

"I...I wasn't thinking of that," Jackson said. "The connection. The victims. Obviously, I shouldn't be gloating over finding a possible answer when my own mother..."

Tess wanted to reach out for him then. Put a hand on his arm. She settled for softening her voice and saying,

"I'm also happy we might be on the same track. It doesn't mean we're okay with what happened. Or that we forget who it happened to."

He nodded, his gaze still lowered. "You're right though. My mother must have been one of the subjects. She went for help and ended up there and..." He swallowed. "Killed herself. During or after, it doesn't matter. Obviously, they didn't cure her. They may have made her worse." A few minutes passed before he looked up sharply, cursing as he did. "Your—I'm sorry. I don't mean to be...I'm not the only orphan set on this trail, which means I'm not the only person affected. Your mother...or your father..."

"One must have also been a subject. Maybe my mother for the same thing. Depression after she had me."

"Or because of your power. Retrocognition. That has to come from somewhere. If *you* thought it might be a sign of mental illness, there's a good chance whoever in your family had it thought the same. That would be a reason to seek help, and then possibly end up in an experiment like this."

"I guess so."

"We need to find out exactly what was going on at Sainte-Suzanne. It seems as if it wasn't a school-funded experiment, but the people involved did have a connection to McGill. If it's only been sixteen years, they should still be alive to answer questions once we have proof. We can make them answer. My parents will help with that. For now, I'll start asking around—"

"No," she blurted out. "You have to be careful. If this wasn't a sanctioned experiment, then you can't go asking people about it. You saw how that research assistant acted."

"I don't mean I'd go surveying the psych department, Tess. I'll be careful, and I promise I won't bring your name into it. I'd never put you in danger like that."

"Then don't put yourself in it either. Please."

He glanced over at her then, and there was an odd look in his eyes, almost hopeful. She realized her words could be interpreted as *I've moved past all that other stuff*, so she hurried on. "Just because I'm upset over what you did doesn't mean I'd ever want anything to happen to you."

That hopeful look vanished, replaced by such sharp disappointment that she cursed under her breath. Where was the middle ground here?

"Let's just get back to this," she said. "There's no reason we can't work together civilly. Maybe we're not adults, but we can act like it, right?" She smiled a little when she said that, trying to lighten the mood, but his gaze only shunted away, his mouth tightening.

"I don't want to work together civilly, Tess. I want to know what I can do to make you forgive me."

"I—"

"I like you." A flash of something like mortification in his eyes. "I don't mean I like—of course, I like..." He seemed to get tangled in his words and slowed down. "I think you're great. You're..." He struggled for a word. "Interesting."

His face flushed. "That sounds stupid. You're lots of things, and I like that. You're pretty and—" Another look of horror. "I shouldn't start with that. Obviously you're pretty, but it's not the most important thing, but you're also smart, and you're funny, and—" He took a deep breath. "Let's just go back to the beginning. I like you."

He met her gaze and waited.

"All right..." she said.

"That means I don't want to be business partners, Tess. I want to keep getting to know you. I want to be friends and maybe if..." He trailed off. "I like you."

"Is that what you think I want?"

His face screwed up. "What?"

"You're trying to figure out how to get me to forgive you. You think that's how to do it. Tell me nice things. Say you like me. Because I'm a girl, and you're a boy, and you're cute, so naturally, that's what I'd want to hear."

"I'm not—"

"Can we drop it? I'm allowed to be upset by what you did, Jackson. Pretending you like me is only going to make it worse."

He shot to his feet so fast it startled her. He walked three steps. Then he turned and threw up his hands. "I can't win here. I just can't win. Do you really think I'm the kind of guy who'd lie about liking you? If I was, wouldn't I be a little better at it?"

"I'm not trying to fight, Jackson. I just want to drop this and get some work done."

"We've done enough for today. If you want to do more, see if there's anything you can dig up in the library before it closes. I'm going to do some research of my own—figure out who at McGill might be connected to Hebb and Cameron. Is that good? Is that *civil* enough for you, Thérèse?"

His eyes blazed, but she answered calmly, "Yes. Should we meet up in the morning? Breakfast?"

He glowered, turned on his heel and stomped to the end of the walkway, but he couldn't quite do it, and he paused for a few seconds before growling, "Seven thirty. At your dorm," and then he stormed off.

Twenty-Eight

BY THE TIME Tess got to the library, it was closed, so she spent the evening on a patch of lawn, eating maple taffy for dinner and going through the notes Jackson had made from the journal, summarizing them and adding questions in the margins. Busy work, really, to keep her from thinking about Jackson himself.

She longed to call Billy and talk about it. There were also a couple of the girls she'd like to call, but she had no idea how to reach them, and it didn't really matter, because they'd be as useful—or not useful—as Billy. All would commiserate, but none would really be able to offer her sound advice on a boy.

Jackson certainly wasn't her boyfriend, but aspects of the relationship were the same. You meet someone and you fall for them fast, and then when they turn out not to be what you thought, you're left lost and confused. Regular friendships weren't like that—at least, not the ones she'd had in Hope, where she'd known people forever and friend-ships blossomed slowly.

Had she been too hard on Jackson? She didn't think so, but a second opinion—and third and possibly fourth—would help.

He'd said that fumbling through his declaration proved it was genuine, but that was ridiculous. The fact he'd fumbled with it only proved he'd been making it up as he went along, forcing himself through a lie.

She wouldn't think about that. Or she'd try not to. She worked until dark, then went to bed and...and nothing. She lay there for almost two hours before getting up again.

What could she do at midnight? The answer was obvious. It would be the perfect time to return to Ravenscrag. To seek the answers that had been denied earlier. To conjure up "ghosts" of the past with only a sleepy security guard to stop her.

Tess slipped from her dorm and into the night. It was a short walk to Ravenscrag, but she headed in the opposite direction. Toward Jackson's dorm. She wouldn't do something that could get them both in trouble without warning him first and, hopefully, enlisting his help. If he refused to help, that wouldn't stop her. She just wanted to give him a choice.

The problem came when she reached his dorm. Dorms were cheap and convenient for students, but they weren't hotels. There were rules, and a matron on duty ready to enforce the one that didn't allow visitors this late.

Tess surveyed the windows. If she had any idea which was Jackson's, she could throw pebbles. She peered inside. The matron was reading *Mademoiselle*, though in Tess's opinion, she was a little old for it. Regardless, the magazine engrossed her, and Tess could probably sneak past. Then what? She didn't know Jackson's room number.

Tess opened the front door. The matron lowered her magazine and raised a scowl.

"*Bonsoir*," Tess said. "*Pardonnez-moi...*" She noticed the magazine was the English version and switched language. "My cousin is staying here, and I've had an urgent message for him. Our grandfather is in the hospital and has taken a turn for the worse. My cousin needs to come right away. May I speak to him?"

The woman eyed her, and Tess wondered if her performance had been less convincing than she thought, but after a moment the woman harrumphed and said, "Name?"

"Jackson Labine."

"The Indian boy?"

"Métis, but yes. Could I—"

"He isn't here. Left about a half hour ago."

"Did you see where he went?"

"Out." The matron paused, then relented, adding, "He got a phone call from a man. He took it, went back to his room and then hurried off a few minutes later. It must have been about your grandfather."

Tess thanked her and left. Outside, she walked across the lawn, damp now as dew collected. Where would Jackson go at this hour?

The caller must have been the mystery man. He'd phoned Jackson's home and been given the dorm number.

If he'd called the dorm, he wanted to speak privately again.

Tess looked around. Where was the nearest pay phone? She didn't walk far before she heard Jackson's voice.

"Thank you for this," he was saying in French. "I appreciate it."

Another voice, one that teased at Tess's memory. "You roused my curiosity. I was hardly going to be able to sit in my office after that." The man laughed, and that's when Tess recognized him as Dr. Augustin.

After a moment she saw them crossing the lawn, taking a shortcut between two dark buildings. Their voices carried through the quiet night.

"I apologize for the lateness of the hour," Dr. Augustin said. "I hope you were not sleeping."

"No. Working on this case. I think I found another connection earlier, and I was trying to puzzle it out before I saw Tess tomorrow."

Dr. Augustin chuckled. "Wanted to impress the girl, did you?"

"I...I did something stupid. She's upset with me, and she has good reason to be, so I'm trying to make it up to her. Which is why I'm glad you have more for me. I really want to have something to show her tomorrow."

Tess broke into a jog as the two disappeared into the dark gap between buildings. Their voices drifted back to her.

"I think it is about more than apologizing," Dr. Augustin said. "You are, how do they say it? Sweet on the girl?"

An embarrassed laugh from Jackson. "I don't think they've said it like that in about twenty years. Mostly this is about apologizing for a mistake. A big one."

"Apologizing to a pretty girl is never a bad thing."

"About the case. You mentioned off-campus experiments predating Cameron's work."

Tess reached the gap between buildings. She could see them ahead. She hesitated, not wanting to eavesdrop but not wanting to announce herself either, in case Dr. Augustin wouldn't speak as freely in front of a stranger.

"That's exactly what I'm looking for," Jackson said. "Earlier experiments that weren't linked to McGill. Specifically, ones near a town called Sainte-Suzanne."

"Yes," Dr. Augustin said. "I know all about Sainte-Suzanne."

He reached up and clapped Jackson on his bare arm. Jackson let out a yelp and spun.

"What?" Jackson stumbled backward, staring down at Dr. Augustin's outstretched hand. "Wh-what did you...?" The words came slower now, slurred. Then Jackson collapsed. And the two figures disappeared.

Twenty-Nine

THE FIGURES WERE gone. Which meant they hadn't been there at all. Well, yes, they *had* been, but not now. Sometime in the past half hour, Dr. Augustin had drugged Jackson and taken him...where?

Tess raced to the spot she had seen them and searched for a sign. Even with dew on it, she couldn't see drag marks on the grass no matter which angle she looked at it from.

Where had Dr. Augustin taken Jackson? And why?

The second part didn't matter yet. She needed the answer to the first. But there was no possible way—

Maybe there was.

Tess closed her eyes and focused. She imagined the figures. She ran through the scene in her mind, concentrating as hard as she could, and when she opened her eyes...

She stood alone in the gap between the buildings.

Tess backed up to where she'd been when she saw them and tried again, but it didn't work that way either. She couldn't conjure the past from thin air.

Yet she had in a way, hadn't she? The visions in the basement, then at Ravenscrag and now here, tonight? They weren't random glimpses into another time. They were providing answers she'd consciously been seeking. But now, when she needed an answer more than ever, it wouldn't come, and the more she tried, the harder her heart pounded, her blood racing, a voice inside her screaming that she had to find Jackson, find him now, before Dr. Augustin hurt him.

Think. That's what she had to do. *Stop panicking. Stop relying on visions. Just think.*

She looked around. Where could Dr. Augustin take Jackson? She peered in the direction of the psychology department and then at the distant tower of Ravenscrag. While Jackson wasn't big for his age, he wasn't small either. Dr. Augustin was an old, overweight man. He couldn't drag Jackson far. And if he'd wanted to take him to the psychology or psychiatry department, he could have gotten him into either building voluntarily and incapacitated him there.

Wherever Dr. Augustin had taken Jackson, it was someplace nearby that Jackson would have balked at entering in the middle of the night. Tess looked at the buildings on either side of her. One seemed to be in active use, with a couple of lights on in the upper floors. The squat building to her left had few windows, all of them dark. There was a walkway to a door bearing a sign that declared the building private and warned against trespassing. Tess turned the handle. It opened. She went inside.

Sound echoed so much in the building that she had to remove her shoes and walk in stockinged feet. In the silence, she picked up a low murmur, which she followed toward a closed door. Dr. Augustin was talking to Jackson in an odd, almost soothing way, telling him to listen to his voice, just his voice, to relax and listen. When Jackson responded, his voice was equally strange—monotone and devoid of emotion.

Tess remembered the articles she'd seen in the professor's office. Hypnosis. Dr. Augustin had hypnotized Jackson.

Though the door was closed, their voices became clear as soon as she drew up alongside it. The only problem? They were speaking in French. She closed her eyes and focused, and while she couldn't translate every word, she could make out the gist of their conversation.

"I want to talk to you about the house near Sainte-Suzanne," Dr. Augustin said. "Tell me about the house."

"It's very big. Stone. Probably Gothic Revival."

"Let me be more specific. Tell me what you found there."

"Tess. I found Tess there."

That didn't seem to be the answer Dr. Augustin wanted, but he had Jackson explain how and why Tess had been there. Then he asked how and why Jackson himself had been there. Jackson told him about the mysterious man. Dr. Augustin grilled him, but Jackson couldn't tell him much, and in the end Dr. Augustin dropped it and asked what else they'd found at the house.

Jackson talked about the locked cell-like bedrooms and the boxes with the scratches. Then he told him about the journal.

"Have you read it?" Dr. Augustin asked.

"Yes. I made notes."

"You still have it? The journal and the notes?"

"Tess does."

"Then you will get it and all the notes and bring them to my office tomorrow. You will tell her that I have offered to help. Do you understand?"

"Yes."

"Tell me what you read in the journal and where it led you."

Jackson explained everything. When he finished, Dr. Augustin said, "Your parents always said you were a brilliant boy. I can see why. You take after your mother's side. Your father? How do they say it in English? Not the brightest bulb. Now, when you awake, you will remember nothing of this conversation. You will—"

"You are Dr. K. From the journal. The man in charge. It's not a surname. The K is for Kenneth."

Silence. Then a flurry of French as Dr. Augustin tested whether Jackson was still hypnotized.

"You are too smart, too curious, boy. It will get you in trouble someday. Fortunately for you, I am not in the habit of hurting children."

"You are Dr. K.," Jackson said. "Tell me you are—"

"If you do not calm down, you will awaken, and I will be forced to take action I do not wish—"

"You are—"

"All right. You will not remember what I said anyway. If it keeps you calm, yes, they were my experiments. There was value in Dr. Hebb's work, but he would not continue it."

"Then the experiment was not connected to the university and was done without Hebb's knowledge. It was military."

"One takes research money where one can find it, and my focus was always on the patients."

"Who got worse. Like my mother."

"Your mother—" Dr. Augustin clipped his words short. "I have answered your question, Jackson. I want to know—"

"And Tess's mother? Or was it her father?"

"She has no father. Her mother was unwed. Now—"

"Tess's mother came to you because of her power. Retrocognition."

"She was pregnant, and she feared passing it along. I was not convinced she had any power, so I persuaded her of the truth—that she was mentally ill—and that the best thing she could do for her unborn child was to be cured before the babe was born."

"You enrolled a *pregnant* woman in your experiments?"

Jackson lost his monotone, his voice rising in incredulity before he controlled it.

He's not really hypnotized, Tess thought. He's faking it.

She held her breath, but Dr. Augustin didn't seem to notice Jackson's mistake; he was too focused on calming Jackson down so he could finish his own queries.

"And she was cured," Dr. Augustin concluded. "She left and she had her baby, Thérèse, and whatever happened after that, I do not know. Now—"

"She wasn't fine. She'd suffered serious—"

"Short-term memory loss. *Short-term.* That is the fault of those who helped me carry the treatment out. They lost faith. They saw the *temporary* cognitive effects—and they began to undermine me. When you have a course of treatment, you cannot fail to follow it because you feel bad for the patients—"

"It's *about* the patients," Jackson said. "It is all about the patients, and if you make them worse…" He trailed off, as if realizing his act was slipping. Then he returned to the monotone voice. "I wish to know more about my birth mother."

"I'm sure you do, but I'm not going to tell you." There was a new note in Dr. Augustin's voice now, a slippery, sibilant note, like a hiss.

He's figured it out.

Tess gripped the doorknob and turned it as slowly as she could. She eased the door open a crack as Dr. Augustin continued.

"Tell me, Jackson," Dr. Augustin said. "Have you kissed Thérèse yet?"

"Wh-what?"

"That's not the correct answer, my boy. You are under hypnosis. You must answer all my questions readily and truthfully."

"Tess and I are only friends."

"But you've thought of kissing her, haven't you?"

"I—no."

"You can't lie if you're under hypnosis."

"I—"

A laugh cut Jackson short.

"That was almost ridiculously easy," Dr. Augustin said. "You are such a smart boy, Jackson. So very clever. Unless the answer is not found in books."

A chair squealed. Tess eased open the door to see Jackson on his feet, backing away from Dr. Augustin, who held a syringe in his hand. The professor's bulk hid Tess well enough that Jackson couldn't see her.

"No," Jackson said. "Listen. I—"

"You played me for a fool. That is what you did. Clever, clever Jackson. Not quite so clever, though, tricking a man while your hands are bound behind your back. Rendering you helpless but not silent. That is what the needle is for. Because now I need to figure out what to do with you."

Jackson took another step back. "Hypnotize me. For real this time. Make me forget all this—"

"Too late."

Dr. Augustin lunged toward Jackson. By the time he did, though, Tess had crept up behind him, and as he lunged, she kicked the back of his knee. The surprise attack made him twist to one side, and when he did, he went down. He kept hold of the syringe, his eyes narrowing as he looked up at her.

"That was a very foolish thing to do, Thérèse. You are a foolish girl, like your mother. Quite mad too. Like her. You do not have a special gift. What you inherited from her is madness."

"No, I see—"

"I have studied parapsychology for almost forty years. There is no such thing as psychic ability. Like your mother, you suffer from mental illness, and you will end up like her, having a child out of wedlock and abandoning that child and stepping in front of a car."

Tess stood shocked for a moment. She vaguely saw Dr. Augustin lifting the syringe, and as he did, she snapped out of it and staggered back a step. Jackson was faster. He stomped on the professor's arm hard enough that the man gasped. The needle flew out of his grip, and Tess dove after it.

Tess grabbed the syringe and backed away as Jackson did the same, leaving Dr. Augustin on the floor, cradling his arm.

"My mother is dead?" Tess said.

"Are you surprised? The only sane thing she ever did was giving you up. You are going to end just like her, Thérèse. I can see it now. You are already mad, spouting stories about visions."

"Then it's madness that led me here. I saw you, with Jackson, outside this building. A vision of what you did. That's how I found you."

He gave an ugly laugh. "Then you are a liar as well. If you saw us, it is because you were following Jackson, and now you tell stories to impress him."

"She doesn't need to tell stories to impress me," Jackson said.

He met Tess's gaze, and her cheeks flamed red-hot. She looked away quickly.

"You don't believe me because you don't want to," she said. "It proves you're wrong. That people *can* have psychic powers. It also means you had the chance to prove that with my mother. That would have been a real breakthrough. Real results. Career-making results. So much better than taking money to help brainwash soldiers."

"I never—" He stopped and went quiet, and when he spoke again, his voice was a low mutter. Tess stepped closer. He lifted his gaze.

"All right," he said. "I will tell you about your mother, and you will let me go. She…"

He lowered his voice again. She moved another step, ignoring warning motions from Jackson.

When she was close enough, Dr. Augustin launched himself at her, grabbing for her wrist, but she was ready and jabbed the needle into his arm. His eyes went wide.

"You…" His mouth worked. "You cannot…"

"Yes, I can," she said, leaning over him as he slumped to the floor. "I can also make sure everyone knows what you did to our mothers."

His eyelids fluttered. Then his head dropped to the floor, and he went still.

Thirty

TESS AND JACKSON stood behind the building, catching their breath after racing out.

"What do we do now?" Tess panted. "We can't call the police on him, can we?"

"No, we can't prove anything. We need to take what we know to my parents. They'll figure out what to do next. At the very least, he'll be censured. Probably lose his tenure. Which is a huge deal. The end of his career. I'm not sure if that's justice."

"The truth will be justice."

"About your mother...I'm sorry."

She nodded, her gaze dropping. "It...it hasn't quite hit yet. I feel...It's like you. I never knew her, so it's hard to..."

He reached to squeeze her hand and she nodded her thanks, then said, "Right now I'm just happy for answers."

"I know."

They were quiet for a moment. Then she looked up at him. He was standing in front of her, the two of them tucked into the shadows.

"You knew, didn't you?" Tess said. "When he summoned you out of your dorm. You were planning to trick him. You just didn't count on the sedative."

Jackson ducked his head, hair falling forward. "I, uh, wish I could say yes. That might impress you, but it really wouldn't be getting this whole honesty thing off to a good start, and I think you'd prefer honesty."

"I would."

"I had no idea until I woke up in that room with my hands tied and Dr. Augustin trying to hypnotize me. I've seen him do it before, so I could fake being under. Maybe I should have thought it was odd that he wanted to meet me so late, but he's always been like that. Impulsive and driven. Which I guess explains a lot."

They watched the distant flicker of car headlights before he continued. "He must have befriended my parents to keep an eye on me. Or on *them*. See if they took an interest in my mother's death. Anyway, I didn't see it coming. All that mattered was that he was offering information we needed, and I wanted…" He cleared his throat. "I wanted to get that for you, to show you how sorry I was. But it would have been more impressive if I *had* figured it out in advance."

"I'm still plenty impressed. You got what we needed, and you're fine."

"Thanks to you," he said, meeting her gaze. "You were amazing."

She blushed, but before she could look away, his arms went around her, his mouth going nearly to hers and then pausing, as if expecting her to pull away. When she didn't, he kissed her, a slow kiss that was everything she'd ever imagined a first kiss would be: careful and sweet and a little bit awkward and nothing like in books, but real—very real and very perfect.

When he pulled away, he looked down at her, face just above hers, worry touching his eyes. "Was that all right?"

"I think so. But I might need another to be sure."

He chuckled and kissed her again, more confident now. Then he said, "I am sorry, Tess. I know I handled the Sainte-Suzanne business badly, and then I handled the apology badly, but I'm really, really—"

"I know. Just don't do it again." She looked up at him. "You don't need to tell me everything, but if something *affects* me…"

"I only have one secret, Tess, and that was it. Everything else—"

A noise cut him short. Someone clearing his throat. Jackson wheeled, his back to her, shielding her as a figure stepped from the darkness.

It was an old man with wild white hair. Tess's breath caught when she saw him, and she told herself she had to be mistaken. Then he spoke, and she knew she wasn't.

"Sorry for the intrusion," he said. "But I believe you wanted to speak to me, Jackson?"

It was the man who'd helped Tess buy her scarf that first day in Montreal. As he addressed Jackson by name, her stomach went cold.

Was Jackson still lying? She couldn't believe it, maybe out of näiveté and maybe because he'd just kissed her. But when he turned to the old man, he stared at him in honest confusion.

"I...don't know you," Jackson said.

The old man smiled. "Perhaps not, in the sense that you don't know much about me, but we *have* spoken. Just this evening, in fact. You were supposed to call me back."

Jackson's eyes went wide with dawning realization, and he turned to Tess. "It's the man who sent me to Sainte-Suzanne. When I phoned home tonight, Mom said someone called and left a number, saying it was urgent. I called back from the dorm, and we agreed it was better to talk from a pay phone, and then the professor called and..." He turned to the old man. "Things happened."

"That's putting it mildly," Tess murmured.

"Why don't you tell me about it?" the old man said.

Jackson shook his head. "Not until you tell us who you are and what you want. After tonight, we're not trusting anyone."

"Understandable. I was already concerned you'd uncovered a situation more dangerous than I expected. Walk with me a bit, and I'll step out of the shadows, literally and figuratively."

They headed for the lit path. The old man said, "I had a nephew. He passed on a few years ago. Cancer. In the end... it was terrible in the end. He was in agony and seemed to be losing his mind. He believed the cancer was punishment for something he'd done, some secret experiment from his time in medical school. Before he died, he begged me to find two children. His actions had, indirectly, led to them both being orphaned. He gave me the names and made me vow to find them and tell them what happened to their mothers. Yet he died before he could tell *me* what happened to their mothers."

"He gave you our names," Tess said. "Mine and Jackson's."

"Yes. I found you, and I made sure you were safe and healthy, but it seemed best not to interfere until you were older. I contacted Jackson last year, when he went to university. I wasn't in any rush though. Not to reveal myself or to insist that you investigate your parents' deaths. You're young and you have other concerns, and, in truth, I was hoping to have more to give you before you began. My own inquiries weren't getting me far. Travel is difficult these days." He indicated the cane. "I have"—a vague wave—"health issues."

"You were monitoring that phone number though. For the house in Sainte-Suzanne," Tess said.

"Yes. I'd sent that envelope to the Home, to be opened on your eighteenth birthday. I'd bribed the local operator to contact me if anyone ever called the number."

"You could have just given Tess *your* number," Jackson said.

He smiled. "And deprive her of an adventure?" He shook his head. "I had nothing to tell her. Just an address and old phone number. It seemed best to entice you both with a mystery. Now, if you've found the solution, I would love to hear it. That, however, is up to you. It's your story. My only job was setting you on the path to finding it."

Tess looked at Jackson. He nodded, and she told the old man everything.

Epilogue

One Month Later

TESS WALKED OUT of the admissions office, clutching a folder in one trembling hand. Jackson stepped from the shade of a maple and came to meet her.

"How'd it go?" he asked.

At those words, the kernel of panic inside her exploded. "I don't know. It's so late, and my school record is good, but it's not exactly from a normal school, and the interview seemed all right, but maybe they were just being nice—"

He cut her off with a kiss. "They're never being nice. I'm sure it went well, so I shouldn't have asked."

"What if I don't get in?"

He put his hands around her waist. "Then you have a plan. What is it?"

"Work in Montreal and try for winter-term admission."

"Exactly. And if you wanted to travel instead…" He met her gaze. "I won't hold you back, Tess. I want the girl I met in Sainte-Suzanne, the girl who does exactly as she pleases.

Admittedly, I would hope you wouldn't plan to travel forever, or I might do something stupid, like follow you—"

"I'm not going anywhere. I will one day, but..."

She might not have traveled as far as she'd planned, but she'd found what she was looking for. A future. Not necessarily with a boy. That was nice—very, very nice—but it was like building a house on unstable ground. She had to make her own future. All her life she'd dreamed of traveling, and now she'd done it, and she realized it hadn't been a destination so much as an escape. She'd wanted to get away from Hope and that constricted life. Moreover, she'd feared she didn't have a future, not a long one, that in a few short years the visions and the nightmares would rob her of it, and so she had to do and see everything right away.

She knew now that she wasn't going crazy. Which meant her future stretched ahead as far as she could see. Meeting Jackson and coming to McGill had shown her that she wanted something different. Like Jackson, she wanted to learn. Also like him, she had no idea *what* she wanted to learn. He was just starting to realize that himself, to admit that the path his parents had set him on—to a career in law—might not be what he wanted. They would explore their options together.

The trip to McGill for her interview was only a brief interlude in a busy summer. They'd reported Steve from Sainte-Suzanne, which had meant police interviews. Jackson's father had helped with that. Tess was staying with Jackson's family. They'd insisted she do that while they all unraveled the mysteries of what had happened at Sainte-Suzanne with Tess's and Jackson's mothers.

Tess had learned more about her mother, with the help of Jackson's parents. She had indeed walked into the path of a car. Accidentally, from all reports. Had she been lost in one of her visions? Or was it a result of the experiments—the confusion and memory loss? Tess didn't know, but she'd learn more someday. For now, she had a real name: Thérèse Vaillancourt. A real name and a glimpse into a real past.

Dr. Augustin had been right—there was no father's name on her birth certificate. That didn't bother Tess as much as she'd thought it might. She had her answers. As for her identity, that was up to her. She'd make her own. Discover her own.

"Tess?"

They were walking now through the campus, holding hands. Jackson looked over at her, his brows knitting.

"Are you all right?" he asked.

"*Je vais bien*," she said, stopping and putting her arms around his neck. "*Très bien. Et toi?*"

He smiled. "*Très, très bien*," he said and leaned down to kiss her.

ACKNOWLEDGMENTS

First, thanks to Eric Walters for inviting me onto this project and to my fellow Secrets authors for their patience with my first collaborative series effort.

Thanks to Sarah Harvey at Orca for her help knocking this one into shape.

Thanks to Xaviere Daumarie for checking my French and reminding me about all those accent thingies I really did mean to add…later.

And thanks to my daughter, Julia, for double-checking my research, knowing that while I love to read historical fiction, writing it always makes me nervous!

KELLEY ARMSTRONG is the author of the Cainsville Modern Gothic series and the Age of Legends YA fantasy trilogy. Her past works include the Otherworld urban fantasy series, the Darkest Powers and Darkness Rising teen paranormal trilogies and the Nadia Stafford crime trilogy. She also co-writes the Blackwell Pages middle-grade fantasy trilogy as K.L. Armstrong with M.A. Marr. Armstrong lives in southwestern Ontario with her family. For more information, visit www.kelleyarmstrong.com.

**Uncover more Secrets—
starting with this excerpt from:**

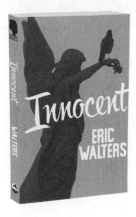

I SAT ON my little bed and took a sip from my cup of tea. The tea was just the way I liked it: warm and sweet with three heaping spoonfuls of sugar. The cup itself was of fine bone china, made in England, so light it felt like air, so thin I could see light through it. Not the type of cup we'd used at the orphanage, where even the toughest cups had seemed to crack and chip.

The house was quiet and still. Everybody had turned in for the night. I felt cozy and safe, tucked into my little room. For years I'd shared a room with Toni, and while I liked being with her, I'd always fantasized about having a room of my own. Now I wished there was a second little bed here, with Toni tucked into it. Wishing wouldn't make that happen. Nothing would. There was only one thing to do to make her feel closer.

I placed the cup down on the night table and picked up the pad and pen I'd put there. Three times I'd tried to write

Toni, and three times my efforts had ended up crumpled and in the wastebasket in the corner. It wasn't that I didn't want to write to her or didn't have things to say to her, but it was still hard to know what to say. After all, I'd spent more time talking to her than anybody else in my whole life, but I'd never written her a letter before. Could I even be sure that she would get it? I guessed there was only one way to find out, and the starting part was easy enough.

Dear Toni,

I hope this letter finds you well. I also hope it finds you and that this letter-exchange system really works. My train ride was very uneventful. What was waiting for me was a little more eventful. I was picked up by a Rolls-Royce, like I was some kind of movie star. What I really am, of course, is a maid for a very rich family. I knew I was going to be a domestic, but I had no idea just how rich the family would be. That must sound naïve— which you've always accused me of being—because it isn't like poor people have maids, but these people are really, really rich. Probably the richest in Kingston. And, if not the richest, certainly the most influential.

They are also a very nice family. There is the matriarch, Mrs. Remington. She likes classical music, like Mrs. Hazelton does. She is kind and nice, and she likes me. Her oldest son lives in the house. He is different. Not that he isn't nice, but he doesn't really get along well with other people. Perhaps that's not correct. He doesn't really understand people and they don't understand him. He spends a lot of time with his pigeons. There is an older son,

Edward, who lives across town with his family. He is the mayor of Kingston and is very important. He is also very nice, and he actually does look like a movie star.

The people I work with—Mrs. Meyers the housekeeper, James the driver, Nigel the cook and Ralph the gardener—are all nice people. They have worked here so long that they all knew my mother. That is the strangest twist. My mother worked here. I lived here as a child and they all knew me and tell me stories now about what I was like. It's very strange and quite wonderful.

I am writing this as I sit in my room. This is the room my mother lived in before she had me, and then we moved to a guest cottage at the back of the grounds. I grew up right here. Who would have ever thought this was possible? It wasn't a coincidence. Mrs. Remington told me that she had a hand in making it all happen. She is a very important person. So important that even the police chief does what she wants.

Sometimes the things they say to me spark little memories. Mostly, though, it's like I'm being told about somebody I don't know or a movie I haven't watched. Still, it is good to know something after knowing nothing. It makes me feel more…

I struggled for the word that would finish the sentence. I thought of a few before I came up with the right one.

…complete. It feels like a hole inside is being filled up.

When Mrs. Hazelton gave me that envelope, the last thing I wanted was to read what was inside. It hurt to find out about *my past, what had happened to my mother. I guess I need to tell you first.*

This was not going to be easy, but I had to tell her. There was no other way.

I came into the orphanage because my mother was killed. The hard part is that she wasn't killed in a car accident or something like that—she was murdered by my own father. They weren't married, but still, he was my father. He was found guilty and sent away to prison.

It was painful for me to find all of this out. I guess I understand why they'd hide some things, but now I just wonder why they would hide so much from us to begin with. Good or bad, or in this case, even horrible, it is our lives, our past—it's who we are. I'm discovering who I am, and while it's strange and frightening and confusing, it is my journey. It feels like I'm reading a book after living a life that started on chapter four. Now I'm reading something about those early chapters. Maybe my mother wasn't a princess, and there isn't any magic to where I began, but it is my beginning.

I wish you were here to share in it and to help me understand it—the way I'd try to help you with what you're discovering. Toni, I truly miss you. You are my best friend. I know, I know, I can just hear you telling me to stop saying the obvious, but I had to say it. I love you so much.

I'm so sorry that we didn't have the chance to say goodbye. For a while I was angry about it, but you know I can't stay angry at anybody for long, so I certainly couldn't stay mad at you.

I've decided we didn't have a chance to say goodbye because it wasn't really goodbye. It's just until we meet again.

I want you to write back as soon as you can to tell me what you've found out, what's happening in your life, what you're doing, thinking, feeling, and when we can see each other again. Kingston and Toronto aren't close to each other, but they aren't that far apart either. We need to arrange for one of us to come to—

There was a knock on the door.

I pulled the blanket up slightly. "Yes?"

The door opened slowly, and Edward peeked in.

"I'm sorry for disturbing you this late," he said.

"It's all right."

"I saw the light on under your door and hoped you weren't asleep."

"No, I was just writing a letter to a friend." I held it up to show him and then instantly thought better of it, as if he could somehow read the line I'd written about him looking like a movie star.

"May I step in?" he asked.

"Yes, of course."

"I didn't want to wake anybody up, but it's only proper to ask formally before entering the bedroom of a young lady. I wanted to thank you for what you did for my brother today."

"It was nothing, really, nothing," I protested.

"It was much more than that. I heard about the altercation. Things could have gotten out of hand if you hadn't been there to provide a calming influence."

"I really didn't do anything."

"That's not what the officer said."

"You spoke to David—I mean, Officer Gibson?"

"David? It sounds like you spoke to him too," he said.

I felt myself starting to blush for no reason. "When he came to apologize, we spoke for a few seconds."

"He met with both me and the police chief." He chuckled. "I must admit, I felt sorry for him. He seems like a nice young man."

"He is. Well, I think he is."

"Just remember, *seeing* nice doesn't necessarily mean that somebody *is* nice. I only wish I could have convinced your mother of that."

The words seemed to leap out of him, and I saw that he instantly regretted what he'd said. He looked embarrassed. I had to ease the discomfort.

"I wanted to thank you as well," I said.

"Thank me for what?"

"For my mother's headstone. I had no idea it would be so large."

"You have to thank my mother for that."

"I will thank her as well, but Richie told me that you were the one who insisted on it and that you wrote the inscription."

"I wish he hadn't told you any of that," Edward said.

"I'm glad he did. What you wrote was beautiful."

"I didn't write those words as much as feel them. Your mother was a very, very special person. She was a kind and generous soul. She was as close to an angel as I've ever met in my entire life. If only…" He shook his head. "I shouldn't be talking about this. I don't want to cause you any distress."

"If it's about my mother, I'd like to know. There's so much I don't know."

I braced myself for something bad.

He looked like he was thinking, choosing his words carefully.

"Your mother was—how should I say this?—an innocent. She believed in people, and she always saw the best in them."

"My friend Toni says that about me all the time!"

"It's not surprising that you not only look like your mother but are like her inside too. Remarkable. Standing here looking at you, having this conversation in this room, brings me back to a time when I was much, much younger." He shook his head. "I just wish, with all my heart, that I could have convinced her that not all people are worthy of trust."

I knew instantly who he was talking about.

"Because she only saw the good in people, she didn't see the evil. I knew it was there. In the end that's what ended her life. If only she'd listened to me and stayed here—stayed away from him."

There was no longer any doubt. He was talking about the man who had murdered my mother. He was talking about my father.

"That's why I need you to understand that not everything and everyone is the way it seems all of the time. Take that young police officer. Perhaps he is not as nice as he seems.

I want you to take measures to guard yourself, and always be aware. Can you promise me that?"

I nodded.

"Not just with him." He paused again, so long that I almost jumped in to break the awkward silence. "I've been told that you're spending a great deal of time with my brother."

"He tells me stories about my mother and me when I was little. He remembers so much."

"He does absorb facts and recite them, but always be careful of the context of those recollections."

I had no idea what he meant.

"You know that he doesn't understand many social situations, right?"

I nodded.

"That means he might know a date or even a time, but he doesn't know anything about what is behind those facts. For example, have you talked to him about what happened with the police officer?"

"No, I haven't."

"Good. In fact, I recommend that you don't discuss it with him, but if you were to, even years from now, he could tell you the day it happened, who was with him, where he was going, possibly even the license-plate number of the police car. What he couldn't tell you was why he was asked to stop, why he shouldn't have walked away and why that could have led to a significant problem."

"After it happened, he told me that he doesn't talk to strangers."

"And he didn't know the police officer, so he wouldn't talk to him," Edward said. "From Richie's perspective that makes perfect sense. Thank goodness our money and position in the community afford him some protection."

"I didn't expect him to do that with the shovel," I said. "He's always so nice."

"He is basically nice, like a child, but there is a part of that child that is always dangerous. He just doesn't understand the consequences of his actions. I feel bad for saying these things. He is my brother, and I'm very protective of him, but I feel the need to be even more protective of you. I can't ever allow anything to happen to you—to dear Vicki's daughter." He sat down on the edge of my bed. "I just wish I had done more. I wish I could replay what happened. I will never stop feeling that somehow if only..." The words trailed away.

I reached out and put a hand on his hand. "I know you did all that you could."

"You really are your mother's daughter. Here I came to offer you my thanks and comfort, and you've been the one who gave me thanks and comfort."

I didn't know what to answer, but it made me feel warm inside—cared for.

"It's getting late. I must go home before my wife gets worried." He got up and went to the door. "Good night, dear Lizzy."

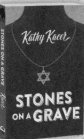

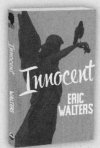

IN EARLY JUNE 1964,

the Benevolent Home for Necessitous Girls burns to the ground, and its vulnerable residents are thrust out into the world. The orphans, who know no other home, find their lives changed in an instant. Arrangements are made for the youngest residents, but the seven oldest girls are sent on their way with little more than a clue or two to their pasts and the hope of learning about the families they have never known. On their own for the first time in their lives, they are about to experience the world in ways they never imagined...